INFILTRATED

MAYA DANIELS

VINCI
BOOKS

By Maya Daniels

Daywalker Series

Investigated

Infiltrated

Instigated

Initiated

Infuriated

Ignited

Vinci Books

vinci-books.com

Published by Vinci Books Ltd in 2026

1

A CIP catalogue record for this book is available from the British Library.
Paperback ISBN: 9781036706739

The EU GPSR authorised representative is Logos Europe, 9 rue Nicolas Poussion, 17000 La Rochelle, France
contact@logoseurope.eu

Chapter One

The night is beautiful.

There is something calming and reassuring when I am surrounded by shadows, the silvery light of the moon shining down but only occasionally caressing me like gentle fingers. The silence is full of mystery and life if you pay close attention to it.

It speaks.

Tightening my arms around my bent knees, pressing my chin on them, I watch the treetops sway in the forest encircling us. The pregnant moon hangs low in the sky, bathing everything in an enchanted glow like a cloud of glittery dust sprinkled everywhere. It would be serene and dreamlike if we are not talking about nightmares. Red and yellow eyes pop up here and there, shifters and demons patrolling the grounds and destroying the illusion by bringing reality into play—a not so subtle reminder that our lives are in their hands. Well, not my life, but everyone else's.

One might think this is a prison, not an academy.

The longer I sit on the windowsill, my spine rubbing on

the harsh stone at my back, the later in the night it gets. The temperatures are dropping, condensing the glass and blurring my view. Everything seems to move further away, my turbulent thoughts fighting for attention in hopes of dragging me down the slippery slope of despair. I don't want to be here, but I can't leave.

I tried.

The moment I came around after losing consciousness at the declaration Soren made, I pushed everyone away from me and bolted out of the building. His words followed me like a curse echoing inside my head. *"I tied her life to mine. And mine is tied to all of yours. If you kill her, you will all die."* That wouldn't have been that bad if he didn't hit me with, *"Welcome to Daywalker Academy, Francesca Drake. Your training and education will begin immediately,"* right before it.

So I ran.

My feet barely touched the ground as I fled through the forest, low branches and tall shrubs snagging my skin and clothing as if they wanted to hold me back. I still remember the stinging pain like thousands of papercuts across my skin as my hair streamed behind me, my breaths sharp in my ears. And all that for nothing. The moment I neared the gate, all my strength left me and I crumpled on the forest floor like a marionette with cut-off strings. I can still smell the scent of wilting and decaying leaves and wet soil, as well as the stench of blood soaking the earth under my nose when the skin on my face was pressed on the ground by an invisible force holding me down.

I've never felt so powerless and weak.

The skin on my arms pebbles with the memory of that night a week ago. Zoltan's arms wrapping around me and lifting me to his chest is the only pleasant memory, and it only makes me angrier. All of them play gods with my life

2

one way or another, regardless of the motivation behind it. Zoltan, Fenrir, Roberti, Soren...every single one of them think they have a right to make decisions in my name.

A weight settles on my shoulders, pressing me down. I know I shouldn't let the thoughts depress me, or I might as well kill myself now. Feeling sorry for myself is not going to get me out of this shitstorm. The more I think about it that way, the less depressed I feel. I can always depend on myself to get out of whatever crap I've gotten myself into. It may not be stealthy or smooth, but it can be done. If there is a body count and blood trail left behind, so be it.

A grin lifts the corners of my mouth.

"You see, that." From the corner of my eye, Fenrir waves an accusing finger at my face. "That look on your face right there...it tells me trouble is coming. Whatever you are thinking, you should stop now."

The damn Fae is like a bad smell. I can't get rid of him no matter how hard I try. Wherever I turn, I see him watching me warily, as if he expects me to grow horns or something. Always watching. Always only a few feet away.

Annoying as fuck!

Dread and fear have me in their clutches, their claws embedding deeply into my very soul. But I'll never let any of them see how desperate I am to turn back time and never return home the night I found Roberti waiting for me in my apartment. *Never let them see your fear, Franky.* Reminding myself of that, I allow my grin to grow.

"I don't like it," Fenrir grumbles while I do my best to ignore him.

Huffing, he folds his arms across his chest, eyes narrowed on me like he thinks he can read my mind. Standing in the same spot for the last few hours, he is leaning on the wall next to the window, head tilted to the side so he can look at my face. In the darkened hallway, if it wasn't for his platinum hair neatly tied at the base of his neck and the golden glow of his skin, he would blend in with the shadows wearing his long-sleeved black shirt and black pants. The golden emblem—a dragon sitting on top of his left pectoral—is like a hot poker in my eye. I hate it as much as I hate Roberti right now.

"You can't ignore me forever."

"I can try." Finally giving in, I pull my gaze from the misty window and lock it on his. "Anyone told you that you are as annoying as a mosquito on a hot summer night?"

"I'll have you know that females have never complained about my company." If possible, his eyes narrow further, turning into slits.

"I'm pretty sure none of them had their life ripped from their hands at the time, either." Okay, so it is a shitty thing to say, but it's not like he didn't ask for it.

Flinching like I just physically slapped him, the Fae drops all pretense, his face softening and shoulders slumping in defeat. My own stiffen, knowing what's coming next.

"Francesca, no matter what I say and how many times I apologize, I can't change anything that has already happened." With a sigh, he rubs his fingers over his forehead. "We screwed up. All of us. No one expected for any of this to happen."

"I don't want to talk…"

"And instead of pushing all of us away"—He continues talking like I haven't said a word—"you need to stop for a moment to hear us out. We can't change the situation, but we can turn it to our advantage."

Pressing my lips in a firm line, mostly to keep my mouth shut more than anything else, I glare at him. As if that is me encouraging him, he gets animated, pushing off the wall to face me better, his arms waving around with each word. The silver light of the moon washes over his face, giving him an ethereal look too perfect to be mistaken for anything else but an immortal.

"Think about it." Reaching for my arm, my scowl deepens, and Fenrir stops an inch before making contact. "As bad as it looks, they played with open cards thinking they had all of us cornered. No one expected Soren to even stir, much less speak. It gave us the upper hand, and now we know who's behind some of the problems we are facing. Would you rather run, or would you rather take advantage of it, destroy them, and stop whatever it is they are planning on doing?" Dropping his arm limply to his side, his fist clenches and a muscle ticks in his jaw. "Intentionally or not, Soren gave you an opening you can't just throw away. For all our sakes, you must see this for the opportunity what it is."

"Don't you dare lecture me, Fae!" Hissing, I bare my fangs at him, forcing him to take a step back. His eyes widen comically, and I realize I've moved, poised on the windowsill on my hands and knees ready to pounce on him. "Who should I look for that is planning something? You? Zoltan, Roberti, the Board, Soren…? There are too many of you and only one of me. What would you have me do?"

I know that I'm not fair to him, or Zoltan for that matter. They did prove whose side they were on the day my life went to shit…well the day my life got more screwed up than it already was anyway. But I can't help being defensive and bitter.

They all lied.

"You need to let him talk to you." Shaking off the initial reaction to my aggression, Fenrir squares his shoulders.

And there it is.

The reason the Fae follows me around like a lost puppy through the floors and hallways.

Zoltan.

An unfortunate-for-him side effect of having his blood in my veins is that I can feel the vampire whenever he gets near me. Not a few feet or anything. I can feel him from a few yards away, thankfully. It helps avoid crossing paths with him, even if it makes me look insane when people see me fleeing through the building like it's on fire. Knowing that he can't come in the hallway leading to Soren's room is a perk I take advantage of all the time. I don't know the reason why he can't cross whatever invisible barrier exists, but I don't question it. Maybe the old-as-dirt Soren has a twisted sense of humor and loves torturing Zoltan. I wouldn't put it past him.

"I have nothing to say, Fenrir." With a sigh, I settle back down on the windowsill, the scraping of fabric against wood filling up the quiet space around us when I shift my legs to curl them under me. "I still haven't processed everything. Until a day ago, all I was capable of doing was screaming 'oh shit' in my head. I'm sure even an old fart like yourself can understand that." Smirking at his glare, I lean my head back, looking at him through half-closed lids. "I need time."

"We don't have time." Pushing the words through clenched teeth, the Fae looks ready to drag me kicking and screaming to do what he wants me to do.

"Says the immortal." I can't help it when the corners of my lips tilt up at his pissed-off face.

"Long-lived and immortal are two different things. Not all of us have eternity." His mouth snaps shut audibly, and I see his breath gets caught as soon as the words are out of his mouth.

"What does that mean?" He got my full attention with

his slip up, my heartbeat speeding up at the implications of it. "You're not planning on dying, are you?"

"You won't get rid of me that easily, I assure you." Fenrir winks, but I notice his fists clenching when he thinks I can't see it.

"I know I'm not that lucky. You and that damn vampire are like a curse I'll never be rid of." There is no fire in my comment, yet Fenrir stiffens regardless. I watch him for a long moment before deciding to drop it and let him be for now. Judging by the way we are looking at each other, neither one of us is in the mood to go down that rocky road.

Glancing down the empty hallway as if expecting someone, Fenrir locks gazes with me before breathing out a deep sigh. "I have a class to teach."

"Hurry along then." Flicking my fingers in a shooing motion, I grin at his frown. "Go annoy someone else. I could use five minutes of peace."

"Please don't get in trouble while I'm gone." Looking down his nose at me, he transforms in front of my eyes. From Fenrir, the guy following at my heels, to the royal Fae that expects all of us to bow at his feet. "I'll find you when I'm done."

With that, he spins on his heel and saunters down the hallway, leaving the scent of forests and rain in his wake. I watch him walk away, his broad shoulders swinging with each firm step he takes, his clothing molding to his body like a second skin. Thanks to a certain vampire, it does nothing for me, but it still should be illegal for any man to look the way Fenrir does. Good thing they keep him here away from human women. Can a female go insane from seeing perfection? I hope we never have to find out.

"You can come out now." Still looking in the direction

Fenrir disappeared, I blow out a slow breath. "He won't be back for at least an hour."

"You knew I was here." Astara comes out of the shadows as if she's stepping through a portal from another realm. "How? Not even the Fae was aware of my presence."

Shrugging a shoulder, I turn to look out the window, my eyes following a drop of condensation trickling down the glass. "I don't know…" my voice trails off, and Astara slides on the windowsill opposite me, curling her legs underneath her just as I have mine, our knees touching slightly.

"You want to talk about it?" Her voice is soft, and I see from the corner of my eye that she's looking out the window too, her hair falling over her shoulder covering most of her face.

"No."

"You want me to leave?" Her body shifts slightly, telling me that if I say yes, she will honor my wishes and disappear as fast as she appeared at my side.

"No."

"Okay." Leaning her head on the wall behind her, she gets more comfortable. "If we get interrupted in pretending we don't see each other, I got it. I'll rip their throat out."

"You're angry?" Feeling bad that I've ignored her for no other reason than the fact that she is related to Zoltan, I almost continue talking, but her laughter snaps my mouth shut.

"Angry?" Still chuckling, Astara bumps her knee to mine in a weird nudge. "No, I'm just hungry."

A burst of laughter comes from me, echoing and bouncing off the walls around us. Shaking my head, I finally relax my shoulders, the tense muscles of my back loosening the knots that were giving me a headache. Leave it to a vampire to disperse tension by mentioning violence.

Chapter Two

My fists clench when I push my hands further into the pockets of my pants. Pressing my elbows close to my sides so I can avoid any contact, I wade through the throng of people rushing to get to wherever their next class should be.

Studying is the last thing on my mind.

After Soren's declaration that I'm a student here, clothing magically appears in my room, filling up a closet the size of my apartment back in Sienna. Mostly the same black ensemble everyone else is wearing, but there are a few colorful pieces that scream Fenrir from a mile away. The Fae thinks he is sneaky as shit, but I'm onto him and his antics.

Not that I'll tell him that.

Also, every second day, there is a cup of fresh blood waiting for me, one I'm yet to summon enough self-control to refuse. I can smell Zoltan's essence in it as soon as I open my eyes, making my mouth water and fangs descend until they are throbbing in my gums. Like a feral animal in bloodlust, I attack it each time, slurping and licking the walls of the glass. It should be freaky knowing he can enter my room even though the door is always locked while I sleep, but surprisingly it doesn't bother me as much as it should.

I won't tell the damn vampire that I'm onto him, either.

Astara, on the other hand, just hangs around me the second I'm alone, not saying a word. Apparently, it's our thing now, sitting next to each other in utter silence. It's strangely comforting, so I welcome it. I did tell her as much before resuming our mute get-togethers.

"Which class?" A familiar male voice pulls me from my thoughts, my head snapping sharply in his direction. Jerking back, he lifts both hands palms up in surrender, but a huge grin blossoms on his face. "Just asking because it seems we are going in the same direction."

I narrow my eyes at the wolf shifter I had the unfortunate pleasure of meeting at the gates when I took on the stupid mission that got me in this mess. His hair flops messily over his high forehead, almost dropping over his yellow eyes. I can see his animal lurking in the depth of his gaze, as if it doesn't want to miss anything. The prickly shadow that seems permanent over his square jaw gives him a roguish appearance.

We tried to kill each other then.

Nothing has changed now. I still want to kill him, despite his handsome face.

"Half of these people are walking in the same direction." Grinding my teeth, I turn away, staring ahead at nothing in particular. "Go away."

"I think we started off on the wrong foot." Undeterred, he falls in step with me, even when I try my best to leave him behind by walking as fast as I can without running. "I was only doing my job."

"This matters to me why?" Dodging people left and right, I tangle my fingers in the fabric of my pants so I don't wrap them around his neck. "I'm not here to make friends. Go away!"

"Listen." Keeping his voice conversational as if I haven't spoken, he glances quickly around us to see if anyone is paying attention before moving slightly closer to me. "Guards, and those like me, hear lots of things…" his voice trails off when we pass a couple of demons, their red eyes zeroed in on me burning with hatred. I grin widely at them, loving the glares I receive in return. "Things you might want to know in case someone, let's say, tries to set a trap for you."

The wolf gets all my attention, my shoulders stiffening at the warning in his words. My feet slow down, and my head swivels to look at him. Like he hasn't said a word, he looks ahead, walking unassumingly by my side. Nothing to see here, folks. He just threatened a half blood.

"You need to work on your threats, pup." I surprise myself with the malice in my softly spoken words. "Bigger and badder things have tried to kill me, yet here I am, dealing with a fleabag like yourself."

"You misunderstood me, Francesca." I can tell I pissed him off, but I must give him credit for not snarling like I can tell he really wants to. "It wasn't a threat; it was a warning."

"What? We are friends now, and you give a shit what happens to me?" Chuckling humorlessly, I resume walking, leaving him lagging for a few moments.

"You are the one acting like a pup." He catches up quickly. "Reacting on instinct and lashing out when you are cornered." I can see him shaking his head as if disappointed. "I expected more from you."

"You don't even know me." Cringing at the defensiveness in my tone, I bump into the person walking by me, causing her to take a step back as she stumbles out of the way. "Sorry..." murmuring under my breath, I tighten my elbows even closer, almost causing pain in my back.

"True," my new buddy chirps from next to me. "But I do hear things, as I said. I've heard a lot about Agent Drake from those in Sienna. What I see now..." his voice trails off, and he gets the reaction he was hoping for.

I give him an expectant look, and that stupid smile makes an appearance again. "Well?" Growling the question, I hate that I ask but am completely unable to stop myself.

"I see a wounded pup." Going back to the analogy I used on him, his smile grows at my scowl. "Unlike the fierce and formidable female that most of Sienna are wary of. You should be picking your allies and forming a plan. Instead, you are trying to bite the hands that are reaching out to help you. Not a smart move." His head bobs up and down like he agrees with his own statement. "Not smart at all."

We are passing one of the giant stairways leading to the second floor, and I use it to my advantage. Grabbing the shifter by the arm, I yank him under it, slamming his back on the wall as I get in his face, teeth bared in a snarl. His fingers wrap in a punishing grip over my upper arms, his nails digging in my skin.

"Listen to me, wolf." Our faces are so close that if anyone sees us, they'll think we are about to kiss with our noses almost touching. "I don't need your help or any information you want to share. I'll say this only once. Stay away from me if you want to keep breathing."

His fingers tighten and the wolf comes closer to the surface, searching my face through his eyes. I can feel the sharp points of his claws poking holes in my shirt as he wrestles with his animal to keep it in check. If I want to call myself smart—even though most already know I'm not—I shouldn't have done what I did. Aggressively manhandling a shifter is not what you do, not unless you want them to tear your throat out. He might have a point that I'm lashing out with no reason, but that's beside the point. It's how I deal with things out of my control.

"What are you afraid of, Francesca Drake?" His deep voice rumbles, vibrating through his chest into mine where we are pressed close together.

"I fear nothing, you fool." Pushing off of him, I whirl around to leave, but he jerks me back, still holding onto my arms.

"That is not true." Those yellow eyes are too knowing, causing my spine to stiffen. "You fear yourself." The shifter's head tilts to the side, sending a sharp ping through my chest. "Well, what do you know. You are a lot smarter than I gave you credit for."

"Remove your hands." Pushing the words through clenched teeth, I feel that telltale sign of calm loosening my muscles and slowing down my heart.

Whatever it is that the shifter sees in my face widens his eyes, and he drops his hands like I burnt him. His reaction snaps me out of the trancelike state that almost pulled me under, forcing me to suck in harsh breaths through my nose.

"Don't touch me, wolf." My throat feels rough when I speak, and I swallow in hopes to moisten the dryness. "Instead of wondering if I'm smart, you should think about your own actions." Turning away, I stop right before coming out from under the stairway. "They can get you killed really fast."

Leaving the shifter behind, I join the throng of people, blending in with the sea of bodies moving through the halls. His gaze follows me for a long time, the feeling of being watched raising the short hairs on the back of my neck. I'm not surprised when Astara joins me, falling seamlessly into step with me a minute later.

"Problem?" she asks casually, as if we've been having a conversation for a while.

"For his sake, I hope not." The jackhammering of my heart that she can no doubt hear clearly calls me a liar. Wisely, Astara doesn't mention that little fact. Neither do I.

"Listen," she says reluctantly, and I turn to look at her when she pauses for too long. "I know we have our thing going on here..."

"You mean hanging out while pretending we don't see that the other is around?" She snorts ungracefully at that, and I chuckle.

"Yeah, that thing," she mumbles.

A guy I've never seen before blocks our path, and I stop along with her. With an athletic build and as tall as she is, his pale skin and phantom-less eyes tell me he is a vampire. A scar runs from his eyebrow and disappears in his chestnut hair, which pulls my eyebrows in a frown. Supernaturals don't scar. What could possibly have left a mark on his face? I don't get a chance to study him long or ask about it. Astara lifts her hand, fingers outstretched like claws, and wraps them over his face, the blood-red color of her long nails standing out against his skin. Not missing a beat, she moves him to the side, shoving his head none too gently the moment he is out of her way, then she continues walking as if nothing happened. I gape at his pissed off face before rushing to catch up with her.

"But I feel like I should say something about Leo," Astara continues our conversation.

"Who?" Still giving the vampire glances over my

shoulder while he stares daggers at our backs, I almost miss what she says next.

"The werewolf you were snuggling with." Her long, graceful fingers flick in the direction of the tall, winding stairway.

"No, I mean who is Leo..." When what she said registers, I snatch her by the arm, yanking her to a stop. "Wait, what?"

"The shifter..." she says it very slowly like she's talking to a simpleton, her eyes boring into mine as if she is trying to see if I'm all there.

"I wasn't snuggling with him." Glaring at her, I debate if I should punch her when she throws her head back and laughs in my face.

"It sure looked like you were, and someone didn't get the memo before running off to tell my brother." Her smile grows impossibly wide like the cat who ate the canary. "Oh look, Fenrir looks like someone spit in his coffee, too." Giggling, she points over my shoulder.

With dread building in my stomach, I turn very slowly to see what she's looking at. The number of people mulling the halls is significantly less now, and it's easy to see Zoltan and Fenrir marching towards the wolf like some choreographed strategic attack, hoarding him from both sides. The shifter stands unfazed, watching them getting near. He is much braver than I am. If I see those two with murderous looks on their faces like they have now, I'd be bolting out of here so fast that only clouds of dust will be left in my wake. When the wolf turns to look at us over his shoulder, he smiles and winks, and I decide right there that he is actually insane.

My feet move to stop the idiots from killing the poor

guy, but Astara jerks me back by grabbing a fistful of my shirt. "Let them be."

"They'll kill him. Look at them." When she lifts one perfect eyebrow at my comment, I shake my head. "If anyone is going to kill the asshole, it'll be me. I don't need bodyguards."

"As I was saying"—Ignoring the bloodbath that's about to happen, Astara sighs—"Leo is actually not a bad guy. Annoying, yes, but not a bad guy."

"Are you preparing his eulogy? Cause he is about to die."

"Don't be silly." Rolling her eyes, she huffs. "My brother or Fenrir wouldn't have listened to what he has to say until it was too late. By getting you riled up enough to get physical, he got both their attention in a matter of minutes. Brilliant, if you ask me."

"Oh dear fates, you put him up to it!" My mouth hangs open as I stare at her.

"I know." Sniffing primly, she lifts her chin. "I'm too smart for my own good."

"Or for his…" I cringe when Zoltan sends the shifter flying into the wall with a punch to his chest.

I've been avoiding him for so long, my heart is trying to punch a hole in my chest from seeing his handsome face again. Even angry, he takes my breath away, his body moving fluidly like the killing machine he was born to be. My lips part as I watch him pounce on the wolf, keeping him on the floor. Fenrir is not far behind, the Fae contrasting with his platinum hair next to Zoltan's dark strands like some twisted yin and yang animation right before my eyes. I'm about to shove Astara away and go help the poor soul when the fists stop flying and I see the vampire leaning closer to Leo, as Astara called him. Zoltan's head snaps in my direction, his blue gaze locking on mine as if he knows where I am the entire time.

I forget how to breathe.

It feels like an eternity until he looks away and, to my surprise, gets to his feet, lifting the shifter up in the process. I can see Leo's lips moving while he wipes his bloody mouth with the back of his hand.

"Let's go." Astara tugs on my shirt.

"I don't get it." Reluctantly, I allow her to start dragging me away.

"I'm sure we will hear all about it later." Chuckling, she bumps her shoulder on mine. "Males, huh. They settle everything with fists."

"You actually just admitted setting it up. So this is on you, not on the males."

"What can I say." Grinning like crazy, she flicks her hair over one shoulder. "I'm a genius."

"If mad scientists count, sure." Shell-shocked, I stare at her back.

Shaking my head, I follow behind while her laughter turns the few heads still loitering our way.

Chapter Three

My feet trail the path my friend is taking on their own. I can't help but think about what just happened. Did the shifter really have information about someone setting up a trap for me? More importantly, is it that bad that he is willing to suffer Zoltan's wrath just to tell someone what he knows? My skin pebbles at the thought, and even the follicles of my hair tingle in awareness of the anticipated danger.

Astara guides me by the arm, pushing me into a seat, and I blink away my thoughts as I turn my head around slowly, finally noticing our surroundings. Wiping sweaty palms on the fabric of my pants under the small desk that I'm now sitting at, I blow out a slow, deep breath. The room is full to bursting with people, their whispered words creating a cacophony of sound like a hum of a large generator vibrating the air from a distance. The scraping of chairs on the smooth floor provokes a few shouts and curses, while others laugh and giggle at the exchange.

All I can do is breathe to keep the pulse of the ancient

monstrosity that Soren tied to me from rearing its ugly head up. The wolf is spot on, pointing out that I'm afraid of myself. What he doesn't know is this: I'm scared of this thing inside me that feels too eager to jump up and play like a puppy with a new toy. No matter what I do, it's always there in the background, lurking...waiting... I just don't want to find out what it's waiting for.

Not yet.

The constant buzz of sound fades in the background when I notice one of the sections empty, the unoccupied chairs sticking out like a sore thumb in the otherwise-crowded space. I take a breath, turning towards Astara to ask about it, but the words die in my throat when all sound stops the moment the door to our far right opens, a group of around ten people walking in. The air around me charges with anticipation. The anger in it is like a bitter taste on the tip of my tongue. Even my friend stiffens next to me, giving off frustrated energy that batters my skin.

I track the newcomers with my gaze, noticing their fluid movement like they are gliding on the floor instead of walking, their heads held high with barely-contained aggression in every twitch of their muscles with each step they take. My skin tightens from the ancient magic inside me fighting to answer the call, to show them they are not the most dangerous thing in the room.

Grinding my teeth, I watch them cross the space, not sparing a glance to anyone present as they take up the empty chairs at the front of the room. One by one, they lower onto their seats across the room from me, eyes trained in front of them as if none of us exist. Until one set of eyes flicks up and locks on mine. The soulless gaze forces the breath I am holding out of my lungs in a rush.

Vampires.

All of them are pure-blooded vampires, and I recognize the guy staring at me like he wants to reap my soul. It's the same one Astara moved out of her way earlier in the hallway. She must notice I'm about to start asking questions because her hand latches onto my leg under the desk, her nails painfully digging into my skin. I won't be surprised if she makes holes in the fabric of my pants. Her reaction is enough to keep me quiet...for now. But I refuse to be the first one to look away from the jerk that thinks he will intimidate me by staring daggers from his safe place across the room. I hold his penetrating gaze, seeing a muscle jump in his jaw the longer I look back.

My lips twitch when his eyes narrow.

"Oh, good!" a deep, rumbling voice calls out, breaking the staring match I have going on with the pure blood. "All of you are here."

I shoot a raised eyebrow at Astara when I see Argoz stride to the front of the room, dumping a pile of thick, leather-bound books on top of a desk I don't notice until now. She gives me a strained smile, but it's the wariness—or maybe even sadness—in her blue eyes that gives me pause.

Astara is always self-assured, just like her brother. There is this aura of authority around her you can't ignore. Some may call it a charisma of naturally born leaders, but I know better. It's the aura of a dangerous creature your brain perceives as a formidable threat, and your will to live forces you to subconsciously to follow. You are either on their side or you are the prey. It's not something the majority can control.

Unlike me.

It's that uncertainty in her gaze that leaves me quietly searching her face for long moments. I see now that her bringing me here while I am distracted from everything happening in the hallway is not an accident. If it's so important for my friend to resort to manipulation just to bring me here, instead of merely asking, I better pay close attention. As if reading my mind, her eyes flick to the group of vampires across from us before she reluctantly removes the hold she has on my thigh.

"If I say so myself, we've made quite a bit of progress in the last few weeks." Argoz's voice breaks the charged silence in the room. "As many of you know, we had some delays. What, with the attack on one of our portals, as well as having a new student arrive later than most of you." He shuffles the books on the desk until he finds the one he is looking for. "I know many of you would rather be in the physical and mental abilities classes, but all that is useless if you don't understand why you are here."

A chair moves, the legs scraping the floor, and the sound makes me jump out of my skin. I don't realize how focused I am on the ghoul until this very moment. My shoulders stiffen and I glance around, but thankfully no one notices me being startled enough to actually jump slightly off the chair. No one but Astara, that is, because she gives me a worried glance. A slight shake of my head gives her enough assurance to look away.

"As we already covered, after the Purge where many of our own died, the Accord was signed to keep the humans and the supernaturals apart. Many disagree with this." Argoz grimaces as if he tastes something foul, then waves a hand dismissively at all of us. "I've heard it all: that we are not cowards, that we shouldn't hide, along with so much more, and it's not like I disagree…" he murmurs like he is having an argument with himself, and I frown at his strange behavior.

"What is going on…" Astara latches onto my thigh again at my whispered words, and I snap my mouth shut.

"At the time, we had wars of our own to contend with while every species thought they should be the ones in charge, that they should be liaisons between our world and the world of humans." Argoz clasps his hands at the small of his back and paces up and down behind his desk, eyes training on his shoes like none of us exist. "Those were horrible days, and many great people died. Luckily the Fae —" Murmurs that sound like curses accompany his words, and my head swivels so I can see what's going on.

"Quiet!" the ghoul booms, and you can hear a pin drop. "As I was saying, luckily, the Fae decided to share one of their most guarded secrets. It stopped the bloodshed, and it's one of the reasons all of you are here today. They sacrificed a dragon blood, tying his life to this institution, and with that, they created the Daywalkers. The pure bloods, the liaisons between the humans and us. Power is a seductive mistress and requires a strong mind and heart to be kept in check. So that no one can abuse it, the Supernatural Agency of the Accord was created, and now everyone is held accountable for their actions."

My ears perk up at that. Nostrils flaring, I do my best to keep my breathing and heartbeat in check. It'll be foolish to let a room full of creatures with enhanced hearing notice how unsettled and eager you are to hear more. I've always been on a need to know basis with Roberti, and he guarded his secrets more than he guarded his life. Maybe being here is not so bad after all.

"It worked well for centuries." Flicking the thick book open, Argoz slaps his hand on it with a resounding thump, my heart leaping in my throat at the sound. "Until now.

Until one of our own started eroding and destroying what we have worked hard to build, what we have bled to create. So you see...giving you powers or abilities to become more...to become part of both worlds without understanding what all of us have sacrificed so you can have it is like giving a child a deadly weapon before it learns to walk. Power without knowledge is a ticking bomb biding time until it destroys us all." Argoz's eyes take on an eerie green glow as he sweeps his gaze over the room. "And that is why all other studies have been placed on hold until further notice."

"It's all because of her!" The vampire that was staring at me before this class started snarls, jumping off his chair and pointing an accusing finger in my direction.

Shouts and yells, followed by chairs flipping over when people jump up to be heard over everyone else, make me push my own seat away. Knees bent, I turn slightly so I can have only Astara at my back. It's quite a testament to how comfortable I've become around her if, at times like this, I allow her to stand where I can't see her. Glancing at her over my shoulder, I can see she's as surprised by it as I am.

"The Fae are tired of being left in the shadows, so they are sending their half-bloods to destroy us all." A spittle flies out of the vampires mouth, his fangs gleaming in the light of the candles lit throughout the room. His upper lip curls in disgust, and I feel my own fangs throbbing in my gums. "They've always resented being seen as less than us."

The anger that is surging through my veins drains out of me at his words. Confusion clouds my mind, and my knees straighten, my balled-up fists dropping limply by my side. What the hell does he mean by Fae thinking they are less than vampires? My gaze flicks from one shouting face to the next, watching shifters, demons, and Fae screaming at each other, pointing accusingly at everyone else. Just the vamps are standing still, glaring daggers down their noses at the rest of us.

"If you don't sit down this moment, all of you will be going through the trials again." Argoz's voice sounds like the wrath of the gods when it echoes so loud the windows rattle from it.

All sound cuts off so suddenly that my ears are ringing and I am a little disoriented. I can feel Astara's hand on my arm, and as much as I hate physical contact, which she pointedly ignores, I'm grateful she holds me up.

"Miss Drake." Argoz's even tone, as if we were not on the verge of ripping each other's throats out a second ago, startles me enough to lock gazes with him, my own eyes wide like dinner plates. "I didn't know you decided to join us." He flicks his eyes to my right, and a knowing look passes across his face when he sees Astara next to me. "We got a little out of line here, but history always has a way of getting people passionate about something." He grins at me, but his smile does not reach his eyes.

"I don't understand..." Something like panic fleets through his gaze, but I have no time to ask my question or worry about what can make the ghoul scared.

The door bangs open, slamming into the opposite wall with a loud crash. A dozen or so guards rush inside, spreading around the room so seamlessly that between one blink and the next, there is one of them strategically placed everywhere I turn. Astara folds her arms across her chest, glaring at all of them. Even Argoz looks put out by the disturbance. I guess I'm the only confused one.

"Argoz, you are needed in the meeting room." Fenrir strides inside, his shoulders swaying with each step he casually takes, but there is stiffness in his posture that makes my heart skip a beat.

"We will continue the class tomorrow." Forgetting about all of us, the ghoul piles up his books, hugging them to his chest like someone is about to steal them from him. "You are dismissed."

"They all stay here until further notice." Fenrir turns at the room, his lips pressed in a thin line that displays his anger.

"You can keep them wherever you want." At Argoz's flippant comment about all of us, my jaw hits my chest, especially when he waves his hand like he's shooing a fly.

The guards stay like statues, one hand firmly gripping the hilts of swords or daggers in a clear threat that they have no problem using their weapons if anyone moves. I'm one second from releasing the fragile hold I have on my control when the Fae looks straight at me.

"Francesca, I'll need you to come with me." Fenrir lifts his hand palm up, inviting me to take it even though he is a couple of yards away.

I stare at him like an idiot.

"It's about time we get rid of the trash." The jerk from the group of vampires gloats, and all of us turn to look at him.

All of us but Astara.

My friend doesn't give me time to process what is going on before she materializes in front of him, his eyes widening comically before they roll to the back of his head and he drops like a rock at her feet. Not even the guards have time to react to her movement.

"Anyone else like to say something about Francesca?" Astara twirls in a circle, looking around before she wipes her bloody hand off the shirt of the closest person standing next to her. "I didn't think so."

Stepping over the vamp, with a hole as large as her fist

in his chest, she sways her hips and descends the stairs. "He will heal, eventually." The explanation is aimed at me, but the smile does not reach her eyes.

"Come." Fenrir waves me on, and I woodenly move to join him.

"What the fuck is going on?" Hissing under my breath, I hope no one can hear my question.

"There was another attack." Grabbing my elbow, the Fae leads me out of the room, my mind spinning with all the unanswered questions.

Chapter Four

I'm vibrating with frustration while I stew in my own anger. In this damn place, you can't be sure if you're better off hiding in a hole somewhere in hopes that no one will come looking, or moving from one room to the next to see what kind of a new shitstorm has hit the fan. Giving a side-eyed glance to the Fae marching me through the hallways, I decide I should hold onto my questions until we get to wherever he is taking me. At least Astara is trailing behind us soundlessly, like a shadow giving me protection from the back. The way that vampire reacted to my presence unsettled me.

The flames dance around when we walk past them, reaching toward the high ceilings like gnarled fingers, expending and retracting from the stirred air. My skin prickles when a mournful howl comes from the outside, the sound full of anguish and something I can't name. It tightens my chest, making it difficult to draw in a breath. Clenching my fists, my nails digging into the skin of my palms, I bite the inside of my lips to keep my mouth shut. A bad feeling, like some unwanted premonition, crawls up my spine, leaving me drenched in cold sweat.

"In here." Fenrir presses his large palm on a door to our left, pushing it open without releasing the hold he has on my elbow, as if he is worried I might run away. His worry is not warranted, but it still irks me to no end.

"I can walk the rest of the way on my own." Snapping at him, I jerk my arm out of his grip, marching inside the room and regretting it the same second.

Blue eyes lock on mine the moment I step inside the vast space, freezing the air in my lungs. Zoltan's gaze bores into me, intense and knowing, causing all sorts of emotions to fight for precedence. The strongest of them all is my fight or flight instinct, telling me to turn around and run as fast as my trembling legs will carry me. Locking my knees so I don't turn into a puddle, I glare at him like he stole my last cookie.

Fenrir clears his throat, startling the crap out of me, and the jerk chuckles when I hurriedly move further into the room. Astara punches his shoulder hard enough to move him sideways before coming to join me. Now that I've broken the hold Zoltan has on me, I notice three others in the room with us. Seeing the wolf shifter deepens my scowl.

"I came as fast as I could." Argoz rushes in, almost colliding with Fenrir, who is still standing close to the door while rubbing his shoulder. "Oh, sorry, Fenrir. I didn't see you there." Sidestepping, the ghoul closes the door before joining the rest at a long table covered with papers, somehow ignoring the tension in the room, as always. For a predator, Argoz is the worse example of our kind.

Clueless by default.

"The portal was attacked?" Argoz leans over the table, frowning at whatever he saw there.

"No." Zoltan's deep baritone makes me shiver slightly, so I inch closer to keep myself moving in hopes that no one will notice. "One of the guards was killed not an hour ago."

"On the other side?" It's Astara who asks the question that brings everyone's attention to us, and I have to force myself not to slap her. Why can't we pretend we are observing so they can forget we exist?

"No, the guard was killed here." Zoltan's focus is entirely on me, drying up my mouth to the point it's difficult to swallow. "The body was found inside the academy, drained of blood." I blink stupidly at him a couple of times before his words penetrate my muddled brain.

"Wait! You think I had something to do with it?" My voice is shrill, the flustered feeling from the vampire's presence draining from me as anger replaces it. "How dare you, you asshole! I was dealing with that idiot over there." Stabbing a finger at the wolf, I'm barely holding myself back from attacking Zoltan. "Or your sister was dragging me through the building."

"Francesca…" Fenrir takes a step closer to me and my head snaps in his direction. Whatever he sees on my face makes him take a step back, lifting both hands palms up in a placating gesture.

"Don't you *Francesca* me, Fae." Sneering at him, I look at each of them in turn. I know they don't trust me; I don't trust them fully either, but accusing me of murder makes me see red. "If I wanted anyone dead here, they would've deserved it. You can bet your damn lives that I would've made sure everyone knew I did it, too."

"I believe what Fenrir was about to say if you allowed him was that no one thinks you did anything." Zoltan's gaze narrows slightly, and I can't decide if it's anger or lust shimmering behind his eyes. Whatever it is, it makes butterflies wreak havoc in my stomach.

"Oh…" Deflating, I take a deep breath, feeling foolish for my reaction, but somehow, I still manage to lift my chin defiantly at him. "Then why am I here?"

"The guard was found two doors down from your room." Zoltan pauses to allow his words to sink in, and sink in they do, like sharp claws gauging into the spaces between my ribs and making it hard to breathe. "After talking to Leo, we believe that he was coming to warn you."

"Is…" my voice cracks, so I wet my dry lips and try again. "Is this about the trap the wolf was talking about?"

"The wolf has a name." the shifter grumbles under his breath as he frowns at me.

"Yeah, Leo. Makes you sound like a pussy cat, not a puppy as I originally thought." I smirk at his growl, but it doesn't last long. The reality of the situation presses on me like a mountain on my shoulders. "I still don't understand why a Daywalker would want to harm me after what Soren said. Unless they are suicidal…" A look passes between all of them, sending a tremor inside me. "What? What is it that you're not telling me?"

"I think this is a horrible idea," Argoz mumbles under his breath, his broad shoulders hunching as he rubs a hand over his face.

"What's a bad idea is waiting around and giving History lessons while Roberti and Cassius are running amok, planning our demise, ghoul." Slapping both hands on the table, I glare at all of them. "Telling me what I'm in for, while obviously everyone is gunning for my life, is not." Turning my head to the side, I search Astara's face. "You know what they are hiding?" Betrayal stabs me like a hot poker to my chest.

"It's not my place to say, Franky. I'm oath-bound; I'm sorry." She looks like she's about to cry, her eyes shimmering in the golden glow that illuminates the room. It soothes me slightly but not enough. I have to remember not to lower my guard around these people.

"We moved the body, and no one in this room is allowed to say a word until we get to the bottom of this. Am I clear?" Zoltan shoots a murderous stare at each of us. "They didn't have time to hide the body or they would've. If we leave them looking over their shoulder wondering who knows about what they've done, eventually one of them will slip. And we'll be waiting."

"A room full of students knows, thanks to Fenrir." Lifting my eyebrows, I look pointedly at the Fae.

"They heard nothing." Fenrir sniffs, looking down his nose at me.

"Right, master of deception. How can I forget?" Grinding my teeth, I look away from his face.

"Bickering among ourselves will solve nothing." Leo sighs, ruffling his hair in frustration and messing it up. "From what I know, Roberti and Cassius are across the portal. They left a few of their minions behind to keep an eye on things and get their hands on Francesca if the opportunity presents itself."

"To do exactly what? Kill me?" The ancient magic pulses hard against my skin, and every person in the room shudders, their primal sides pushing to the surface.

"Calm her down before we turn this place into a slaughterhouse," Zoltan growls at Astara, his fangs denting his lower lip. Warmth pools in my stomach at his wild expression, and some crazy part of my brain wants to keep pushing until his control snaps. "Don't do it, Francesca."

His softly spoken words are like physical fingers gliding over my skin.

"Or what?" My voice is breathy, daring him to finish his threat.

"Ummm, Drake..." Argoz clears his throat uncomfortably, and I see him tugging on the collar of his shirt like the fabric is choking him. "Astara and I can't hold off all five of them."

His comment makes me look at the other males in the room. Fenrir and Leo both, just like Zoltan, have barely-contained aggression plastered on their faces, their bodies poised ready to pounce, and all of them are turned towards me, same as the other two that I've ignored until now. Swallowing thickly, I push the magic brewing in my chest with everything in me until I can feel it retreating. The charged air disperses around us, and everyone sighs from it.

"If not to kill me, then what is their plan? To lock me up?"

"There are worse things than getting killed, Drake." One of the unknown people speaks for the first time.

"Who are they?" I sound like I've been choking on smoke for a day, but I tilt my chin up at the two males that are hesitant to meet my eyes.

"My betas," Leo answers, rolling his shoulders, I assume to release the tension in his muscles that all of us feel.

"I still stand with what I said earlier," Fenrir says before I have the chance to ask more questions about the shifters. "She needs to know the truth, and we need to move her away from here."

"Finally, someone is making sense." Clenching and unclenching my fists, I pointedly avoid looking at Zoltan. I can feel his gaze on me, unsettling me to no end.

"I'll have to agree with Fenrir. It's not safe for her here, even if we have her in sight at all times," Leo pipes in, the other two shifters nodding their heads in support of their alpha.

"I can go back to Sienna." The idea that I can get the hell out of this place fills me with so much hope I'm surprised my feet are still on the ground.

"Sienna is even worse." Argoz shakes his head sadly, killing my happiness.

"I don't understand." Still staring at the ghoul, I point an accusing finger in his face. "And you are a killjoy, just so we are clear."

"Duly noted, Drake," he tells me dryly.

"I'll make you a deal." Zoltan snaps my gaze away from the ghoul. Excitement and dread battle inside me when my eyes connect with his.

"What kind of a deal?" heart jackhammering in my chest, I hold my breath, ignoring Astara's snort. I can't hide how my body reacts to the vampire at the moment, not even if my life depends on it.

"You move and take the room between Fenrir and me." My mouth opens so I can argue straight away, but he lifts a hand, stopping the words at the tip of my tongue. "Hear me out, then argue." Pressing my lips in a firm line, I nod once, not trusting myself to speak. "You move and you train for two days with us." He circles his forefinger between all the males in the room, tightening my stomach. "After that, I will tell you everything. And I'll take you where you can see that all of it is the truth."

We stare at each other for a long time, none of us relenting. It's almost like everyone in the room is holding their breath, waiting to see what will happen. You'd think all their lives are hanging on my answer, which is ridiculous, of course. As crazy as it sounds, I'm not that worried about the training part. Pain I'm familiar with. I'm freaking out internally about being in close proximity to Zoltan. Having only one wall between us is not enough for my peace of mind. What's worse is that looking at him right now tells me he knows it, too.

His lips twitch slightly at the corners, sending a sharp ping in my stomach. My entire body clenches from that barely perceivable gesture. His smirk grows the longer I look at him.

"Come now, Francesca. I might start thinking you are afraid. You don't trust me, or you don't trust yourself?" The asshole grins, the tips of his fangs poking from under his lip. The problem is there is no humor in that gaze. His too-blue eyes are smoldering with barely-restrained hunger that almost brings me to my knees. "I dare you to prove me wrong."

"Fine!" My ego rears its head before I have a chance to stop myself from answering. "It shouldn't be me that's afraid, vamp."

Fenrir snorts, coughing to cover it up when I turn to glare at him. Astara snickers from next to me, as if the two of them know some inside joke that the rest of us are not privy to. The shifters turn to each other, talking in hushed whispers, no doubt coming up with plans on how to make my life miserable in the next two days. Only Argoz still stands in the same spot, his head turning from me to Zoltan with a calculating look that I don't like at all.

"I'll help her move," Astara says so cheerfully I almost think we are moving in together as roommates, not offering to drag my ass next to her brother, who really isn't good for my health.

"You do that," Zoltan tells his sister, not looking away from me.

"Okay!" Clapping her hands, she takes hold of my arm, bodily removing me from the room. "We'll be going now. You boys be good."

She keeps chuckling like some evil witch from one of the human shows I watch, pulling me with her through the door. Before she closes it, I turn to look over my shoulder. Zoltan's gaze follows every move I make. The door hides him from my view, but I feel that look following me everywhere I go.

Chapter Five

"This was the stupidest idea ever." Throwing a handful of shirts with a lot more force than necessary inside one of the bags Astara has brought, I glare at them like it's their fault I find myself in this situation.

"You'll live." She giggles, pulling them out and folding them neatly. "I have a solution to the problem, but you don't listen to me."

"There is nothing funny at the moment." My words are muffled while half of my body disappears between the hanging garments. "I liked you better when you didn't say a word."

"I would think you'd appreciate being protected after that guard was killed a few feet from your door." Her smile slips from her pretty face, and her solemn gaze locks on mine. "All joking aside, I'm planning on moving close to those two, as well."

"Perfect! You can have my room." My hand stills the pants hanging midair between the closet and the bag.

"Umm, no. I would like to stay alive. Zoltan will kill

me." Shaking her head, the traitor snatches the pants from my grasp.

"I still don't get why anyone would want to kill me." Astara opens her mouth, but I continue talking. "Hear me out. If they are a threat, it means they are Daywalkers. Because if they're not, I'm perfectly capable of looking after myself. I've done it my whole life." The guilty look on her face stops my venting. "What's that look for?"

"Franky, I wish I could tell you everything…"

"Yeah, yeah, the oath, I know." Huffing a breath, I turn back to the closet, yanking stuff off the hangers.

"It's only for two days. You'll know everything then." She looks so hopeful when I glance at her over my shoulder that I feel like crap for taking my frustration out on her.

"I know." Sighing, my shoulders slump in defeat. "I know you are right. It's just after everything that happened, my patience is wearing thin. It's not like you guys owe me anything, I got myself into this mess."

"To be honest, I'm glad you did." My head snaps in her direction, and Astara gives me a sad smile. "I don't want to think what could've happened if they found out what you are without Soren around. The board might be useless nitwits, but they'll never go against his word."

"You think they have nothing to do with this?" Turning to fully face her, I can't hide the shock inspired from her words. "I find it hard to believe they are not in on Roberti's plans. For him to waltz in like he did, someone had to let him in through those gates, and it most definitely was not a guard."

The memories of that night hit me like a battering ram to the chest, and I plop down on the floor next to Astara. The crippling betrayal I felt looking at Roberti's face while he laughed at my naivete to blindly trust him. Zoltan's unconscious body being dragged by the demon guards, his blood pooling on the floor and spreading like an ominous shadow devouring my soul. Cassius looking down his nose, not an ounce of regret for stabbing his friends in the back. The feeling of my own blood being pulled back up my veins to stop me from bleeding on Soren's outstretched palm. It all presses in on me until I can't breathe, and it feels like my ribcage is being crushed, preventing me from taking a breath.

"Franky?" Astara's voice sounds far away, like she is calling my name from miles away.

Looking up, my heart skips a beat when I can almost see the pores on her otherwise flawless skin. Thin blue veins fork out under it, pulsing slightly with each pump of her heart. Her pupils dilate when we lock gazes, spreading into the sun-shaped form I've seen in Zoltan's eyes. Her hand shoots out and grabs mine, crushing my fingers into a punishing grip.

"Franky, please. I can't control myself. Stop!" Her panicked voice snaps me out of the oppressive thoughts, and I suck in a deep breath like I've been underwater for too long.

"What the fuck was that?" Gasping for air, I hold onto her hand to stop myself from falling apart.

"Your eyes changed." Astara sounds as freaked out as I am. "You were pushing me to give myself to my instincts. All I could think about was how much I wanted blood." Her words are frantic, the hand holding mine trembling. "I've never felt bloodlust like that in my long life."

"Great. I'm going to turn all of you into feral animals just by breathing." Panting to slow down my racing heart, rivulets of sweat sliding down my hairline and my spine. "Maybe it'll be best for all of us if they just kill me."

"Don't say that!" Astara snaps at me, jerking me upright from the slumped mess I am on the floor. "It's not just your life on the line anymore. You can't be that selfish."

"I never asked to be responsible for everyone." Her words are like knives to my chest, and I sound defensive. "I didn't ask for any of this. All I wanted was to keep the people in Sienna safe."

"Well, now you have the chance to keep all of us safe." Her punishing grip loosens, and she squeezes my fingers reassuringly. Her emotions flood into me, and I know she's being sincere. "You can do this, Franky. I know you can. Just let my brother and Fenrir protect you until you are ready to fight whatever it is on your own."

"I'm tired of fighting." The words escape me before I can stop them.

My eyes flick to hers, and the confusion I feel is mirrored on her face. Until this very moment, I didn't realize just how real those words are. Ever since I can remember, I've been fighting. Fighting to survive, struggling to move up the ranks, fighting to protect...

"I don't know how to do anything else but fight." At my softly spoken statement, the look in Astara's gaze softens, and she shocks me more by pulling me into a bone-crushing hug.

"You'll be okay, Franky. You'll see." Her body is shivering, and she tightens her arms. "All of us will be okay."

"I hope you are right." My words are muffled in her hair, and I reluctantly hug her back. "But something tells me it'll get a hell of a lot more worse before it gets better."

We both startle when someone knocks and pushes the door open without waiting for an answer or an invitation. Fenrir pokes his head in, his platinum hair falling like a curtain over his shoulder. The frown on his face is fast replaced with a teasing grin as he pushes the door all the way open and walks inside like he owns the place.

"I think I deserve one of those, too." Spreading his arms wide, he makes grabby hands at us.

"A kick in the nuts is what you deserve." Grumbling under my breath, I detangle myself from Astara's arms. "I didn't invite you to my room."

"Since you'll be moving within the hour, technically this is not your room anymore." Looking down his nose, he flicks his fingers in an invitation, still expecting a hug. "My shoulders are starting to cramp, hurry up."

"He must be on drugs." Lifting off the floor, I look down at Astara.

Her face is turning red from holding her laughter in, and I forget what else I am about to say when an awareness starts creeping up my body. It starts at my toes, and like a heatwave, it crawls up so fast it's as exciting as it is unnerving. With it, an idea to see the Fae suffer for a bit comes to me, and I turn towards Fenrir, grinning from ear to ear.

"You are right, Fae." Taking a step closer, I spread my own arms. "You deserve a hug, too."

All humor leaves his face, his eyes widening comically in panic, but it's too late. I latch onto him like Velcro, not releasing my hold even when he tries his hardest to push me away. The air stirs when the door is forced open again. My grin widens so much that my cheeks hurt from it. One second, I'm squeezing Fenrir like a boa constrictor, and the next, the Fae is yanked from me, slamming against the wall.

Zoltan jerks me next to him, his shoulders bunched up and fists clenched at his sides. There is a menacing growl rumbling deep in his chest as he stares daggers at the dazed Fenrir, who only shakes his head as if to clear it. So I don't laugh out loud, I bite my lips so hard I can taste the coppery flavor of blood on my tongue. Checking on Astara, I see her turning almost purple from holding it in as well.

"Fucking females. Evil creatures." Fenrir snarls, glaring back at Zoltan, and that's as much as I can handle.

I burst out laughing so hard, my throat hurts a second later, and tears stream down my face. Astara joins me, both of us curling up on the floor with arms folded across our middle. When I can finally open my eyes, the confused look on Zoltan's face brings another fit of laughter, and it keeps going until I feel so tired I can't even lift my head off the ground. Rolling it to the side, I see Astara is in the same predicament, and we both laugh weakly at the mess in front of us.

"You want me to give you a hug, too?" Astara chirps, lifting her arms towards Fenrir like a child expecting to be picked up.

"I feel like I've been played," Zoltan grumbles, his eyes dancing with mirth.

"We invited the Devil to our table by putting these two together." Pushing off the floor, Fenrir runs his fingers through his tangled-up strands. "This is what I get for coming to offer help."

"The two of you are too predictable. That's not on us." Astara helps me up while I wipe at my eyes. "I can't remember the last time I've laughed this much."

"Very funny." The smile lifting Fenrir's lips contradicts his frown. It's like his face can't decide which emotion to display, doing facial gymnastics in the process.

"Are you ready to move?" Always the man of few words, Zoltan looks around at the already packed bags. I've never had this much stuff in my life.

"Not really, but it seems like I don't have much of

choice." Twirling around, I check to see if I've forgotten to pack something.

"You can always move to my room," he says so casually that the rest of us turn to gape at him. Even Fenrir. "What?"

"You can grab the bags on the bed, Fenrir." Astara changes the subject, allowing me to take a breath. The damn vampire will be the death of me one of these days.

"Right…" Pulling an elastic band from around his wrist, the Fae ties his hair in a low ponytail and snatches three bags like they weigh nothing.

"I'm right behind you." Astara does the same, leaving only one bag behind when she follows Fenrir.

Panic makes me trip over my own feet as I snatch the remaining duffle and rush out of the room after them. I don't make it two feet when thick fingers wrap around mine, buckling my knees. Zoltan wraps a hand around my waist, holding me up, and I can feel his breath tickling the short hairs that have escaped my braid.

"Careful, Miss Drake." My skin prickles with goose-bumps when his lips graze the shell of my ear. "You'll trip if you don't watch where you're going."

"I'll trip." My brain short-circuits from his nearness, and I repeat his words like an idiot. I want to slap myself when I hear his chuckle. Or better yet, slap him to stop him from chuckling.

"What am I going to do with you, Francesca?" He nuzzles my hair, the scruff on his jaw catching strands of it on his face.

"Nothing." I sound panicked as if this right here is a make or break deal. Summoning as much self-control as I can, I push him away, square my shoulders, and start walking again with my head held high.

My heart jumps in my throat when he reaches for the bag again, his fingers lingering longer than necessary on my hand. He pulls it out of my grasp and moves a couple of steps ahead of me, his long legs eating the distance much faster than mine.

"That's where you are wrong." He throws me a look over his shoulder, the permanent smirk on his lips nearly making me trip again. "I have many somethings planned for you."

No matter how much I want to tell him to dream on, both of us know I can't resist him for much longer. But I'll be damned if I don't try with everything I have. My eyes stay glued on the movement of his body, the way his shoulders sync with his hips, and the way his thighs stretch out the fabric of his pants with each step. My focus so intent on the vampire, I nearly miss the silvery glint coming toward his head from around the corner.

Chapter Six

Fear for Zoltan's life gives me a lot more strength than necessary, so when I throw myself at his back, both of us end up crashed at the dead-end of the hallway in a tangle of limbs under the window. A dagger sinks deep into the wall where Zoltan's head was supposed to be, the hilt vibrating like the string of a guitar around us. He stiffens at the sound, and the air thickens so much I'm finding it challenging to fill up my lungs.

A hand is pressed between my shoulder blades, keeping me plastered on the ground when he flips his body, bending over me like a shield. I'm well protected, but that leaves him open for pointy, sharp things to get stuck in him like a pincushion. That thought doesn't sit well with me. When I feel my heart slowing down and the familiar calm blanketing me like a mother's embrace, I succumb to it willingly.

Thump.

Sliding from under Zoltan's arm, I twist up into a crouch by his side. The orangey glow of the flames illuminating the hallway brightens, opening up the shadows and giving away their secrets. I can still hear the trembling of the dagger in the wall, as well as the slow, steady beats of Zoltan's heart. Holding my breath, I place a hand on his upper arm, my fingers tightening so I can get a better grip. And then I wait.

Thump.

In slow motion, from the corner of my eye, he turns his head so he can look at me. At the same time, a shadow expands in the adjacent hallway, and the stirring in the air gives enough warning of the next attack. The coward throws another dagger, the silver blade glinting as it flips through the space headed for Zoltan's chest. Shoving him away as hard as I can, I push off the balls of my feet, sailing through the air and catching the sharp blade between my fingers. Cocking my arm, I send it back to where it came from, the resounding thud telling me it hit the target before my feet touch the ground again.

Thump.

Making sure the vampire is out of sight—albeit with a glower on his handsome face—I plaster my back to the wall, as close to the opening as I can. My arm tingles when Zoltan steps next to me, the heat from his body penetrating through my clothing. Holding my breath, I strain to catch any movement or a heartbeat, the monstrosity that lives inside me now eager to find a target so it can practice. After a long-stretched moment, a scrape on the floor—a misstep that will cost the idiot their life—gives me the exact position of our second attacker. Waiting it out feels like an eternity, and I'm grateful Zoltan says nothing.

Thump.

Taking one running step into the connecting hallway, I bounce off the opposite wall with my foot, twisting my body in the air, and I come face to face with a very startled demon. His eyes widen when we lock gazes a second before my fangs drop from my throbbing gums and I sink them deep in his throat. The force from my body colliding with his flings us both on the ground, my legs wrapping around his torso as we go down, and I squeeze as hard as I can with my thighs. I can hear his ribs cracking under the pressure while he gurgles from his ripped throat. Another dagger is clutched in a large hand, now stretched lifelessly next to his head. The air stirs at my back.

Thump.

Unwilling to release my prey, I flip around and crouch over the dead demon, hissing at whoever is trying to sneak up on me. Coming face to face with a startled Zoltan jolts me out of the feral bloodlust that is driving me insane.

Blinking a couple of times to clear my head, dread numbs me when I feel the blood dripping down my chin and over my chest. Keeping my gaze on Zoltan is the only thing stopping me from losing my shit right now. He stays still, searching my eyes, one hand pressed firmly on the ground between his feet. To my shame, I realize he is poised to tackle me if I try to attack him. Not that I blame him. I can only imagine how I look, covered in blood, hissing, while bent over a dead demon.

"Francesca." My name rolls off his tongue, and the slight accent that sometimes slips when he is not paying attention makes it sound a lot prettier than it has any right to be. "We need to move. I need to know you're with me."

"I'm fine." My voice is hoarse, like I've been screaming from the top of my lungs for hours. When he keeps looking at me as if I might go into hysterics at any minute, I glare at him. "I'm fine. You shouldn't sneak up on me like that again."

"I'll remember that." His lips twitch, the smirk fighting

to pop out only deepening my scowl. "We need to move you to a safe place, come on."

I let him pull me to my feet, following at his heels with our fingers intertwined, the blood making them stick together like glue. It's as disturbing as it is hot as hell, sending all sorts of inappropriate thoughts flying through my head. When my thighs start getting slick, I know it's just a matter of minutes before the scent of my arousal hits him. Zoltan may act like he doesn't notice things, but he will never let me get away with something like that.

"You know they were not trying to get to me, right?" In hopes of keeping him busy enough that he won't pay attention to scents and smells, I tug on his hand to get him to look at me.

"Of course they were." A line forms between his eyebrows when he glances at me.

"Actually, they were aiming at your head." He stops walking so suddenly I bump into his back. "First at your head, then at your heart. With silver daggers."

"Silver can't kill me." There is a barely-contained anger in his words and every line of his body.

"No, but it can keep you out long enough so they can snatch me away." Giving him a taste of his own medicine, I smirk at him. "If I was the type that's easy to snatch, that is."

"Is that why you kept shoving me away?"

"What did you think it was? Foreplay?"

"I can play rough." One side of those full lips cocks up, and I know in this moment that even a human with a sinus problem could smell my arousal, and probably from a mile away. The jerk is not playing fair.

"It was very ballsy of them to try and nail you with a couple of daggers." Clearing my throat, I look at his chin to avoid seeing the knowing expression telling me he is aware that I'm changing the subject. "I would expect them to pull that on the Fae, or Astara..." my words trail off, and my eyes snap to his.

Both of us turn and bolt down the hallway, Zoltan still holding onto my hand, forcing me to run faster than I can remember being capable of. My free arm throbs in pain from slamming it on walls when we turn corners, so I don't do it with my face. I'm not sure I take a breath the entire time, at least until Zoltan almost rips a door off the hinges, and both of us rush through it like Tasmanian devils on crack.

"What the fuck, Zoltan!" Fenrir snarls, his eyes flicking from their usual bright blue to red with white pupils before going back to normal. His hair changes from platinum blond to midnight black, like a picture on a TV with terrible reception.

Taking a deep breath so I can speak, I'm about to point it out... but expanding my lungs lets me know I have something very sharp pressed at my ribs. Turning my head slowly to the side, I meet Astara's pissed-off glare.

"Making shitty moves like that could get you both killed," she tells me pointedly, putting slight pressure on the knife she is holding.

"At least you are both alive," I rasp, and they finally notice that I look like some psychopath that bathes in the blood of her enemies.

"What the hell happened to the two of you?" The sharp point of the weapon disappears, and Astara walks around me to look at both of us.

"They tried to hurt Zoltan." Ignoring his glower, I push past his sister and plop on the one chair in the room. "I'm not sure if they were trying to incapacitate him for the time, or if they really have no clue that their silver daggers can't kill him."

"Did you recognize them?" At Fenrir's question, I flick my gaze to Zoltan's face.

"I didn't stop to look." Spearing his fingers through his hair, he grabs a handful of it, tugging it in frustration. "I wanted Francesca out of the open. I'll check on them now."

"I'm coming with you." Fenrir is out the door before he is done talking, Zoltan right on his heels.

The sound of a key being turned when the door closes is like a bullet in the silent room.

"You okay?" Astara kneels next to me, face turned up, her gaze flicking between mine.

"I'm fine." Blowing out a breath, I sag deeper into the chair. "With the adrenaline pumping, I didn't have time to not be fine." Her hand hesitates above mine, so I take it, squeezing her fingers to let her know I'm telling the truth. "I was scared for Zoltan. They didn't try to hurt me, both of them were focused on him … Even the weapons were not meant for me. They were silver, not iron."

"You are half vampire…" she trails off when I scrub a hand over my face.

"Neither silver nor iron can kill me, Astara. Iron weapons might slow me down or hurt me long enough so I can be killed, but on their own … well, they are useless." Yanking on the braid, I remove the elastic band tied at the end and push my fingers through it, unraveling the long strands. "After Zoltan said silver can't kill him either, I thought they were trying to slow us down so someone could get to the two of you."

"We didn't see a soul on our way here." Sitting down on the floor, she hugs her knees. "You'd think Cassius and Roberti would know what can and cannot hurt my brother."

Her eyes are unfocused as she nibbles on her lip, but that comment gives me a pause.

"You think the Board is involved? Since they can't touch me, they'll go after you now?" I don't know why I didn't think of that sooner. Those three might not dare to go against Soren's word, but the ancient Fae didn't say anything about the ones helping me.

"I don't think so." Astara waves a hand dismissively, her pretty face scrunching up in disgust at the mention of the old farts, as she likes to call them. "Those three are powerful enough together—for now—to not need help from demons. If they wanted the job done, they'd do it themselves."

"For now?" Latching on to the one offhanded remark, I turn my full focus on her face, and I don't miss her flinch, letting me know it is a slip up as I think. "Why do I feel like I walked into the middle of a war when I crossed those gates?"

"Everything will be clear to you in a couple of days." Pushing off the floor, she looms over me. "Now, I think you need to wash off all that blood because you look like you're about to go feral on me at any given moment. Not an attractive sight, I assure you."

Remembering I look horrible, still tugging on the strands of my hair that are tangled and sticking together from the dried-up blood, I stand also, my eyes roaming the length of the room for the first time. A twin bed is pushed in one corner, and next to it sits a side table with a chandelles flame sitting atop of it. A partly open door to the right leads to a bathroom, the tiles on the floor giving it away even when I can't see far inside it. A large window with sheer drapes stands between the bed and a small fireplace, the chair I was sitting on is placed in front of it. A little coffee table low to the floor is piled up with my bags. Another door is facing the bathroom from the opposite wall, one I'm assuming is a closet.

Simple and minimalistic.

I like it.

"You can keep looking after you clean up." Astara's voice sounds strained, and I turn to look at her with a frown.

My eyes widen when I see she's taking small sips of air through her mouth so she doesn't have to smell the blood. Groaning at my own stupidity, I rush to the bags, yanking on the zippers and shuffling the neatly-folded clothing inside. Pulling out what looks like comfy lounge pants and a long-sleeve top—all in black because fates forbid they let anyone wear a different color here—I rush to the bathroom slamming the door closed behind me.

"I'm sorry." Like an idiot, I raise my voice as if she can't hear me through the closed door, I peel the crusted-to-my-skin clothing away. "With everything that happened, I didn't even think about how the blood would affect you."

"It's not the blood that's the problem." She sounds strangled, probably still holding her breath. "I can control myself around blood. There is something different about the one you're bathed in."

"I didn't bathe…" Scoffing at her choice of words, I almost skip the critical part of what she said. Jerking the door open, I lean in so only my head is sticking out of it. "What do you mean 'there is something different?' I had my fangs in that asshole's throat as he bled out. There is nothing different about his blood."

"You can't sense it?" Astara frowns, her arched eyebrows dipping low over her eyes. With her hands on her hips, she lifts her chin and takes a long, deep sniff in my direction.

Her eyes flash such a bright blue they look white as she

stumbles back and clutches the chair behind her. Startled at her reaction, I duck inside the bathroom, closing the door with a slam, even going as far as leaning on it.

"No, I can't sense anything different. What is it?" Lifting my arm, I sniff at it gingerly, and in the same second, I feel stupid.

It's not like the scent has changed. If I couldn't smell it a moment ago, chances are I won't be able to now either. Thumping my forehead on the door, I groan.

"Actually, hold that thought. Let me wash it off, and then we can talk." My skin pebbles from having the dried blood on it now that I know something is wrong with it. I shiver when I turn, and flakes of it crumble down on the pristine tiles.

"Sure," Astara calls out. "I'm not going anywhere until those two come back."

The mention of Zoltan and Fenrir makes my heart skip a beat. How long has it been since they left? Were there more demons waiting for them back there? Anxiety eats a hole in my stomach, and I almost trip when I rush inside the shower.

Chapter Seven

My skin feels raw from the harsh scrubbing I give it, the scalding hot water dimming my natural golden glow. After roughly wiping the leftover moisture from it with a towel, I stab my legs in the pants as fast as I can. My head and one of my arms are pushed through the holes of the shirt, but I'm already yanking the door open, my gaze searching the room for Zoltan and Fenrir.

Stupid, I know.

I can feel Zoltan even if he is not very near, but I can't help hoping I might've missed the awareness of him because of my turbulent thoughts. The room is silent; only Astara stands in front of the large window gazing through it with unfocused eyes.

Seeing her like that stops me in my tracks. Unlike her infuriating brother, she is always animated. Even when standing still or being focused, there is always some tell about how she feels or what she's thinking. Right now, none of it is evident, with her arms folded over her stomach like she's hugging herself, and the way she stands so unmoving you could mistake her for a beautifully sculpted statue. Midnight hair, glossy like oil, spills over her shoulders, starkly contrasting against her alabaster skin and making her red, pouty lips look like freshly spilled blood. She's not even blinking.

"They're not back yet." For some reason, my words are but a whisper, my movements slower as I pull the shirt over my chest.

Astara blinks, drawing away from the thoughts pulling her under their spell. Turning her head slowly, she takes a deep breath and shakes off whatever had her in such a defensive pose. With a smile, she moves away from the window, coming around the chair and plopping on it ungracefully.

"They'll be here any moment. My brother likes to be thorough when he is looking for something." Tilting her head, she grins at me. "At least you look normal again. Well, normal for you anyway."

"Who was the male?" Seeing her so lost in thought makes my own mind run on fast forward. Ignoring her lighthearted comment, I blurt out one of the things that has been bothering me.

"What male?" Her eyes narrow slightly, the smile slipping from her face.

"The pure blood." Grimacing at the dumb explanation, I gather my hair over one shoulder, twisting it to squeeze out the excess water. "The vampire in Argoz's class. First, he tried to get your attention in the hallway, where you literally shoved him out of your face, then you ripped a hole in his chest. That male."

She purses her lips, eyeing me warily. With no intention of dropping the subject, I pick up one of the bags, dropping it on top of the bed. Keeping myself busy will stop me from worrying about why the two idiots are not back yet. Focusing on the task at hand, I put my stuff away, giving Astara the time she obviously needs to provide me with the answer I seek. I was smart enough to hide my acquired knives and daggers before anyone noticed, so I'd rather unpack myself than risk anyone finding them. They may say I stole the weapons, but I like to say it is compensation for all the ones I lost—along with my bike—the day I walked inside this cursed place. If I sound peeved about it, it's because I am.

"He is the son of Silas." Astara finally speaks, her words forcing me to look at her, my hands gripping the shirt I am pulling from my bag and stopping midair. My arm hovers for a moment before I come back to myself and toss the clothing on top of the pile I made on the bed.

"And Silas is?" My left eyebrow lifts in an arch at her thinly pressed lips. Clenching my fist out of her sight, I wait patiently for her answer. With these people here, it's like pulling teeth with my bare hands. "Listen, I know that it'll take time for you to learn to trust me. If it makes you feel better, I don't trust anyone either. But since we are all stuck here, any information that will make things easier on all of us will be much appreciated."

"This has nothing to do with trust, Franky." Leaning forward, she presses her forearms firmly on the armrests of the chair. "That male is trouble. You want some naked truth and a piece of good advice? Stay as far away from him as possible. And to answer your question, Silas is the vampire member of the Board."

"And you thought punching a hole in his chest was smart?" My mouth hangs open as I stare at her incredulously.

"It's one of the perks of being what I am. I guess," she

adds as an afterthought. "I could do without hearing anymore temper tantrums about it." Her hand waves the air in front of her, dismissing my shock. "I hate that I can't speak openly because of the damn oath. And before you start thinking I'm somehow honor bound to these assholes, I should tell you that I physically can't talk about it. It's like the moment I want to say something, the thought disappears, and I have no idea what I was talking about."

"Very convenient." Disappointment is evident on her face at my comment, but she can tell there is no real anger in my words.

The truth is, Soren, tricked me into an oath too. One that I refuse to think about. In my mind, if I ignore it enough if will disappear. Plus, now really isn't the time to think about things I can't change. Instead, I need to deal with whoever is trying to kill me—and everyone else for that matter—right now.

"Listen." With a tired sigh, I stop fussing with the clothing and meet her eyes. "If I have to wait two more days to be told all the secrets being kept from me, I'm good with that. This whole thing just makes me feel like I'm chasing my own tail." Nibbling on my lip, I search her face. "My entire life was a lie. I took everything for granted, and all the things I had in place to keep me centered, to make sure my feet stayed planted on the ground … it was all ripped away. I'm not a trusting person by nature. Never was. So this whole thing … it just made everything worse."

"I know, and there is nothing I can say that will make it better." Leaning back on the chair, she smiles sadly. "But"— She lifts her forefinger in the air—"remember that most secrets are kept for a good reason. I'm not sure if what you'll hear will make things better or worse. At one point, I believed that this"—After she gestures around the room with her arms, her eyes fall on mine again—"what we do here, what we are ... I thought it was for the good of all of us. Lately though, not so much."

Mind spinning with everything she isn't saying, I run the tip of my tongue over my teeth, watching her through slanted eyes. As far as warnings go, this is a very vague one at best. Everything has already turned into a shit pile of epic proportions, so how much worse can things get?

A soft knock on the door has me twirling to face it, arms lifting while my knees bend slightly, ready for combat. From the corner of my eye, I note Astara standing from the chair, soundlessly moving out of sight. My lips part and I take slow, even breaths through it in hopes I won't give my position away. That's the last thing I need if the visitor behind the door is a would-be assassin.

"It's me." Fenrir's voice is muffled through the walls.

Dropping my hands to my sides, I stride forward and yank the door open. Astara pops out of the closet the same time as the Fae steps inside my room. Not wanting to look eager to see Zoltan, I give Fenrir a once over, making sure he is not bleeding or anything before turning expectantly at the still open door. An empty hallway meets my gaze.

"Oh, excellent." On the balls of his feet, Fenrir spins in a circle, a smile plastered on his face. "You've cleaned up the war paint." I blink at him, unable to believe that is what he's focused on, but I notice Astara poking her head out the door, probably looking for her brother. Fenrir only lifts one eyebrow at me in reply.

"Did Zoltan get lost on the way back, or did you leave him dead in one of the hallways?" My chin dips down to my chest as my gaze bores into his. "When two people leave and only one returns, it's usually one or the other."

"He is waiting for us in the training room." Frowning at

me, he folds his arms over his chest. "It'll take more than a couple of guards to take one of us down."

"If I didn't push his ass out of the way, they would've taken him down already." Pointing the obvious out through clenched teeth, I return his scowl.

"Children." Astara steps between us, lifting both arms to ward us off. "Let's not fight with each other, huh? It took you long enough to return, Fenrir. The least you can do is tell us why you came back alone."

"My apologies, I didn't think you would be that worried." His earnest expression deflates the anger painting my vision red.

"I wasn't worried." My face feels warm, and I turn away from them, unwilling to let them see me embarrassed. "I have questions and need answers. After you tell me what I need to know, both of you can do whatever you like."

"Right." Astara dry washes her hands after a thunderous clap. "Let's go see what Zoltan found out. I don't know about the two of you, but I'm not a big fan of swimming blind." When I look at her over my shoulder, she rolls her eyes. "You know what I mean."

"Actually, I don't." I deadpan, almost high-fiving myself, as I watch Fenrir squirm.

"This night seems like it's dragging on forever." Shaking her head, Astara heads out the door. "Everyone is prickly and on edge." Her voice trails off the further she gets in the hallway.

"After you." Fenrir lifts his hand in a gentlemanly gesture, and after giving him a long glance, I head for the door. "I really didn't think you were that worried," he continues conversationally, following me out and closing the door behind him. "I know you are still angry, and I realize you avoid us even on the best of days, so I should've been more thoughtful."

"Very poetic of you, Fae. Just because I don't want any of you dead doesn't mean I like you around." Fenrir chuckles, falling in step with me, but I can't get myself to look at him.

My heart picks up a beat now that I'm out in the open. My gaze searches the shadows, every flick of the flames sending a jolt through my spine. No matter how nonchalant they all seem, only an idiot will take this situation lightly. I haven't been here long, but I know Zoltan is essential to the academy. If they dared to go after his head, it's not just a couple of guards being stupid, even though that is exactly what the Fae wants me to believe.

"One of these days, you'll admit it, Franky." I raise an eyebrow in question, and he continues. "That you can't help but care for me." Fenrir chortles when I turn to glare at him.

"Don't hold your breath on that one." He keeps snickering, so I decide to change the subject because I'll stab him with something if he keeps it up. "You think Astara will get in trouble for attacking Silas's son?"

"Zoltan will take care of it if there is a problem." All humor leaves his face, and I stare at the difference it makes, momentarily forgetting to keep an eye on our surroundings. "Silas is the least of our concerns at the moment."

"I find that hard to believe, but what do I know?" My feet slow down as we reach the vast, open space with giant stairways twisting up as high as I can see. "Ever since I stepped foot here, my concern multiplied."

Fenrir stops me from moving further away when his arm shoots out across my chest, pushing me back a step. Flicking his gaze around, he squints suspiciously at the empty space.

I want to make a jab and give him a hard time about it, but the hairs on the back of my neck are standing on end. Someone is watching us. Someone I haven't noticed.

After a long moment, he shakes his head, lowering his arm. "I could've sworn—"

"Good evening." A deep voice cuts across Fenrir's, coming from the shadows and so close I can feel the air that stirs from his words against my skin.

Spinning on the balls of my feet, I twist around, lifting my leg just enough for my round kick to find its target. My foot connects, jarring my bones with the strength of the hit, but the satisfying grunt of pain I hear is worth it. My fangs drop instantly, and I land in a half crouch, baring them at the person.

A hard thump echoes in the silence when a large, muscled body dressed in black hits the ground on his back. With a loud whoosh, all the air exits his lungs and a pathetic grunt of pain follows it. I'm about ready to pounce on the male while he is still down when Fenrir chokes out a laugh, stopping me in the tracks.

"Sometimes, I wonder why I even bother." Coughing while he struggles to inflate his lungs, Leo pushes off the floor, scowling at me.

"You should know better than to sneak up on me." Shaking off my arms to release the tension, I eye the shifter cautiously.

"I wasn't trying to sneak. I thought both of you knew I was near." Flipping the hair over his forehead, Leo rubs the side of his head before his paw-sized hand moves to squeeze the back of his neck. "I wasn't very quiet moving around, either."

"I don't like this." Fenrir scans the area around us. "Let us move out of the open."

Spinning on his heels, he moves so fast my feet work double time to keep up. Straining my ears, I keep my eyes locked on Fenrir's back, acutely aware now of the wolf at my back. Again, I can't help but wonder how I don't feel anyone around me. My whole life that is the one instinct that has kept me alive.

The hallway we enter is a familiar one, and that's the moment I feel it. A dark, evil presence, like a mountain dropping on my chest. The air thickens, the stench of decay burning my nostrils. My head swivels, hoping I'll catch a glimpse of what or who it is that's giving off the malicious aura, but the two males usher me through the door before I get a chance.

"No, wait..." I rush back out the door, but it's too late.

No one is there anymore.

"What is it?" Zoltan is next to me in a blink of an eye, the heat from his body soaking through every pore on my skin.

Lifting my chin up, I take a long sniff, the clear air confirming my suspicions. Zoltan does the same, sending me a questioning look.

"Nothing." Rolling my shoulders, I turn and head inside the training room. "I thought I smelled something, but I was wrong."

"Let me see what Leo needs and we will start. The sooner we do this, the sooner you will know everything you need to know, and we will put an end to this insanity." He waits until I nod before joining Fenrir and Leo, who are talking in hushed whispers with their heads bent close together.

I watch Zoltan's back as he walks away for only a moment. My gaze is pulled to the now-closed door by an invisible force and dread pools in my stomach. Whatever is out there, it is powerful. Powerful enough to give the magic inside me a pause and to disappear without a trace, much faster than even a vampire can move.

Is it really someone there, or is it some twisted premonition making me feel things that don't exist? Astara coming up to me brings me to the present, and I give her a strained smile that she returns in kind.

Chapter Eight

With sweat dripping over my eyes, I lift my head slowly to scowl at Zoltan. The permanent smirk on his full lips has fury pulsing through my veins because he manages to bring me to my knees.

Again.

And not in a good way. The asshole slams his mind fuck into my skull with everything he has after I gloat about being able to block him now. My fingers curl like claws, the nails digging in the cushioned floor so hard that I'm not surprised to see them bleeding when I glance down.

I'm not sure how long we've been at it. The males said two days of training, but somehow, I have a feeling they lied. The fuckers have me writhing in pain, every second of it dragging on like an eternity. The Fae and the shifter are not as mean, although my abused body will say otherwise. Even breathing causes my muscles to smart, so I keep it to small sips of air through my lips. Zoltan says it's been almost forty-eight hours.

He lies!

I know he does.

"We can stop now if you are too weak." His deep voice is like bass in my chest, jerking my head up so I can stare at him.

I don't even know I close my eyes, or that my head is hanging listlessly on my shoulders. He says I'm weak on purpose, knowing too well it'll irk me to no end. He is an expert in pissing Francesca off by now.

"I'm good, thanks." I want to act harsh, but pushing the words through clenched teeth makes me sound pathetic. "I'll just grab some water." Shoving my pride away, I crawl towards the corner of the room where there are a couple of bottles left.

He drank the others on his own, grinning at me at the same time.

"If you are under attack, you think you'll have time for water?" From the corner of my eye, I can see his boots keeping time with my pitiful shuffling.

"Good thing I'm not under attack then." It hurts to speak, but I keep my eyes locked on the water bottle. My mouth feels like a desert, my parched throat scraping with each word.

"That's where you are wrong, Ms. Drake…"

"I'm fucking Ms. Drake now? Well, you're a gods damned masochistic asshole." Grumbling under my breath, I miss the rest of the lecture he's giving me.

Zoltan stops.

The charged silence doesn't hit me until I actually slide my hands over knees a couple more times. When it does, my body stiffens, leaving one arm in the air while the hairs on the back of my neck stand on end. It's one of those deer in headlights moments when you know you're screwed but there is jack shit you can do about it. I almost jump out of my skin when the heat of his body wraps around me, each breath he takes tickling my ear.

"Don't push it, Drake." Zoltan growls the words deep in his throat, and I startle myself when I whimper like a fool. His massive body is curled around mine, his palms pressing on top of my hands to pin me in place under him. "I would love to show you how euphoric mixing pain and pleasure can be, but I need you to survive what's coming first. I need a lot of time for what I have planned for you."

"Keep dreaming, bloodsucker." A deaf person can hear my heart hammering through my ribs, wanting to punch a hole and escape. It kills the bravado I'm trying to pull off, but I'm nothing if not determined. "Does that shit even work on females? Or you're so old you've lost your game?" My chuckle turns into a low moan when he presses his face to my neck.

"You think this is a game, Francesca?" The amusement I hear douses the lust filling my head with cotton. "I let you have your time to come to terms with everything that happened. Having attacks left and right changes things. We don't have the luxury to give you time so you can lick your wounds. Lives are at stake, mostly yours. If that was not the case, you would be pinned, naked, just like this in my bed, screaming my name. Everything else might be a game. You naked with me inside you is not one of those things."

His sharp fangs press on my neck, hard enough to dent the skin but not hard enough to break it. My back arches on reflex, and I tilt my hips higher, nestling him better to me. My channel pulses from his words, grasping the air and making me feel empty. Wetness coats my thighs, drenching my pants while I pant as he holds me in place. A feral growl vibrates his chest, and I involuntarily tilt my head to the side, offering him my neck. *It feels so good to be at his mercy,* my mind whispers like a little bitch in heat, and my eyes snap open.

"Get the fuck off me, Zoltan." Using our position to my advantage, I tuck my pelvis in before jerking back as hard as I can, slamming my tailbone into the hard, thick erection that is nestled between my ass cheeks.

The fangs disappear from my neck, as well as Zoltan's body from around me. Scurrying to the side, my head swivels around looking for him. I find him on his knees, hands pressed hard on his thighs and head hanging down. His broad shoulders are hunched, the muscles on his arms twitching from the grip he has on his legs.

"That will teach you to try and force me into a submissive pose." Gasping for air, I eye him warily but obviously can't keep my mouth shut.

His head lifts, that too-blue gaze locking on mine and pinning me in place. His pupils are pulsing, ensnaring me in their depths as I watch his lips twitch, then painfully slow they lift at the corners. It's not an evil smile. Not even a pissed off one for giving him a bruised erection. It's one of those smiles that is a promise. You can never be sure if that's a good or a bad thing, but it gets you all hot and bothered with sweaty palms, and you keep thinking about it despite knowing better.

Forgetting all about my sore and bruised body, I push off the floor, my legs screaming in protest. Zoltan doesn't move, his gaze tracking my movement, and I remember the day in the dining hall where I met Cassius for the first time. I kneed the vamp in his jewels then too, and Fenrir kept telling me to step away from him. Something about Zoltan barely holding onto his control, I think.

Just like back then, I keep eye contact with him, the crazy idiot that lives inside my head, daring him to snap.

Everything around me fades away, the whole world centering on that look in his eyes.

The clearing of a throat snaps both our heads in that direction.

"I hate to be a cockblock, but I think we ran out of time." Fenrir doesn't sound sorry at all for interrupting, but the dull look in his gaze makes the words I want to say die on my tongue.

Moving away from the entrance of the training hall, the Fae scrubs a hand over his face in such a tired way that both Zoltan and I straighten up to watch the partly open door, not breathing. Astara is first to walk through it, holding it open with an outstretched arm. The blood drains from my face when Leo and one of his betas shuffle in, carrying the second beta's lifeless body between them. The shifter gives Zoltan a look so empty that my chest feels tight when I see it. They place the body on the floor, reluctantly moving away from it like he will disappear if they are not physically touching him.

"When?" is all that Zoltan asks, walking up to the dead beta and scanning him from head to toe.

"We were getting things together to leave. He went to check on his mate." Leo's voice is grave, leaving me wondering if he screamed or howled when he found his dead friend. "When he didn't come back at the set time, we went looking for him. We found him close to one of the portals." Glancing from Fenrir to Zoltan, he shakes his head. "There was no blood or any evidence of a fight. He was just there ... with not a drop of blood in him."

A tremor crawls up my spine, dread spreading through my chest and sinking its sharp claws in my lungs so I can't even take a breath. My feet move on their own, bringing me closer as I keep staring at the peaceful look on the beta's face. His skin is graying, losing the pinkish hue he had the last time I saw him. Zoltan keeps his eyes on the dead wolf for a long time before lifting his head and nodding once to his sister. Astara slips through the door like a ghost without so much as a whisper.

"I will take him to his mate. We brought him here in case you could feel something that would tell us what killed him." Leo stares at Zoltan with a blank face. "I can scent nothing but him. At the portal or on his body." Kneeling down, Zoltan moves his head along the length of the dead beta before shaking his head. "I didn't think so. We will be back as fast as we can." Both shifters lift the body and walk out as fast as they came, leaving the three of us silently watching the door.

"The Purge was a nightmare like nothing we've ever seen." Zoltan jerks me out of my destructive thoughts, and I turn to him, confused, not understanding a word he is saying. "They like to tell everyone that the Fae were feeling generous, so they sacrificed for the good of all." He doesn't look at me but keeps his eyes on Fenrir. The Fae stares back without saying a word, and I shiver. "The truth of it is, if they didn't, all of us—including them—would've been slaughtered. What no one talks about is that the humans have an organization that is as old as we are. Their only purpose in life is to exterminate all supernaturals from their world. Hunters, they call themselves."

"Humans, even hunters, killing our kind can't possibly be that easy." It's one thing when two of our kind face each other, but a human doesn't stand a chance no matter what they say.

"They have help." Fenrir scrunches his face at Zoltan's words, as if he smelled something foul and doesn't like it at all. "Some of the old gods were getting lost, losing their powers with the new times. They chose the fanatics and bestowed them with gifts, as they say. If you ask me, it's more like a curse since the humans are losing their souls with time."

"Okay." Dragging out the word, I watch Fenrir pull the door closed and settle next to it, crossing his arms over his chest. My eyes flick from his face to Zoltan's as I wait to hear what this has to do with me, or the dead beta for that matter.

"With the years, their numbers grew, and now they are a formidable enemy that we battle. The hunters are the reason Sienna was created, keeping everyone safe. It was the reason this academy was created as well." Clenching his fists is the only movement Zoltan makes. "Being able to defend ourselves or our kind was most important, but those strong enough to do it, or willing to do it I should say, were only able to face the hunters at night. The Fae changed that—for some of us."

"That much I know. You became Daywalkers." Waving my hand between both of them, I'm hoping to hurry Zoltan along. The shake of Fenrir's head slows down my flopping hand, leaving it hanging in the air. "What am I missing?"

"We became Daywalkers." Zoltan jabs a thumb in the center of his chest. "The Fae, the shifters, most of the others ... they were able to walk the day without anyone's help. Vampires, on the other hand, couldn't. Still can't unless they become a Daywalker."

I snort.

The laugh that is trying to come out sounds strangled, my smile slipping off my lips as I see their solemn faces watching me with unblinking eyes. When they both stay silent, lead pools in my stomach, and I lower to the floor, sitting because my legs can't keep me up from the weight of what I'm hearing.

"So, you lied." I can feel my heartbeat in my throat as I look from the vampire to the Fae. "All these other people risking their lives with your stupid trials to come to this academy are doing it for nothing. For lies."

"After they pass the trials, all of them give an oath and are told the truth. They are not obligated to stay if they don't want to stay. The oath prevents them from telling our secrets. Most of them choose to stay of their own free will." Zoltan tilts his head slightly at my upturned face. "You think they don't want to keep the rest safe? They have families protected behind these portals."

"You said yourself they can walk the day without being in this damn place. How are you manipulating them to be part of this?" The longer the Fae stays silent, the angrier I get, so I lash out at Zoltan.

"They get trained here, become stronger, faster, more capable of protecting. No one is lying to them or manipulating them." I can tell I'm getting to the vamp when he grinds the words through clenched teeth.

"They are rebelling, Zoltan. They are killing each other as well as people in Sienna. That tells me not all of them are happy and willing to be here."

"Some have the idea that a dragon blood will give them some additional powers since it's the reason we walk the day." I can tell it pains him to say this, so I keep my mouth shut. "The hunters have managed to convince some of them to work as spies. We need to fix that."

"You mean the demons?" At his frown, I belt out a humorless laugh. "So far, I've only seen demons determined to kill around here. Well, demons—Roberti and your buddy Cassius. Which brings me to my next question. If the others here can walk the day and don't need to become Daywalk-ers, what in the fates name do they do?"

"They are guards." When I open my mouth to tell him how stupid I think that is, he lifts a hand to silence me. "They protect the portals while training to infiltrate the human organizations and their world. We have them in strategic places where we can control who finds out about us and can stop a disaster before it has a chance to happen."

"And you?" Flipping my hand in a mocking circle to encompass his person, I lift an eyebrow at him. "What do you mighty *Daywalkers* do?"

"We fight the hunters." At the simple words, my heart does a painful lurch, thumping once so hard against my chest that I glance down to see if I'm bleeding.

The silence stretches between us like an unwanted guest, one you are forced to entertain while counting down the minutes until they leave. My mind is whirling from every-thing, and all the hits each of Zoltan's words take on my world. It's almost freeing to watch everything you believe being shattered to dust in front of your eyes. I mean, my whole life was a lie, why would anything else be the truth. Which brings me to the most pressing question.

"So, what does this make me?" I clench my fists so they can't see my trembling hands.

"That we are about to find out." Fenrir speaks for the first time.

"How?"

"We are going across the portal into the human realm." Zoltan's words make me dizzy, and I sway where I'm sitting cross-legged on the floor.

Chapter Nine

I stare at the swirling colors of the portal in front of me like I'm looking at the hungry mouth of a monster ready to devour me. Cold sweat trickles down my back and beads on my upper lip. I've never been this terrified in my life. Well, that's not true. I'm not that scared, really. I'm just excited and worried, unable to decide if this is the best or the stupidest idea I have agreed to follow. *Keep telling yourself you aren't scared, Franky. You might actually believe it,* the silly voice in my head chirps, and I grind my teeth.

"It'll be fine." Astara is trying to soothe my worry, but she doesn't sound like her confident self. "It's nighttime over there right now, anyway."

And that's the bitch of it all. Because I'm half Fae and half vampire, no one knows if I'll turn to ashes when I step into the daylight, or if I'll sprout horns. All of them are trying their best to be encouraging—apart from Zoltan, who just says, "If anyone can do the impossible, it's you, Ms. Drake."

Yeah, we are back to Ms. Drake now.

73

The pale rainbow of colors in the portal swirl and shimmer like I'm watching a soap bubble trembling in the wind on the palm of my hand. I should know. It's incredible what you do to keep yourself occupied when you have no friends because you are a freak. Watching soap bubbles is the least embarrassing one, at least.

"Where are we going again?" Not taking my eyes off the portal, I ask no one in particular.

"We will be dropping into one of their big cities." Fenrir sniffs self-importantly. "Los Angeles, the City of Angels as they call it."

"Angels live there?" Turning my head in his direction, I watch him like a hawk for tells if he is lying.

"No." Astara snorts, making the Fae frown at her. "Humans are weird. They like to make up stuff to make themselves feel better." When both my eyebrows reach my hairline, she laughs. "If they knew how mean those winged fuckers are, they wouldn't be plastering their pictures on everything."

"Are we ready?" Zoltan scowls at us. "I don't think Francesca needs a lesson on humans right now. We need to get going before trouble finds us."

When he takes a step closer to the portal, I take a step back. Pausing, he looks at me over his shoulder.

"Last time I tried to leave this place I almost died, thanks to Soren's little trick. I'm not very excited about testing it to see if the same happens when I cross a portal." Locking my knees together, I force myself to stand still, surrounded by the four of them.

Zoltan turns to me with a worried look on his face, and my heart is ready to jump out of my throat. I guess none of them thought this little adventure through. Both of us look at Fenrir when he clears his throat.

"The magic prevented you from leaving the grounds because you were going to Sienna and you were not under oath. The human realm is different. You will not have a problem going through."

His face and the self-assured way he stands tells me he is stating the truth. Zoltan's scowl deepens slightly, but he turns around and strides through the portal, his body disappearing inside the soap-bubble colors. I'm still not convinced that I'll be okay, so I reach for Fenrir's hand, wanting to touch him skin to skin to see what he is feeling. Before my hand can connect to his, Astara grabs my arm, yanking me along with her through the portal.

My body feels like it's been ripped apart from the inside out. Panic grips me in its clutches, preventing me from taking a breath as I'm literally squeezed through a tiny hole and spat out the other side. Dry heaving and hacking, I bend over, clutching my knees and praying to die for what feels like forever, the long braid swaying on the side of my face like a pendulum. Feeling raw and vulnerable, I let the tears stream down my face and blur everything around me.

The sound returns slowly, and only then can I finally take a full breath. The first rational thought I have is, *Thank fuck I'm not dead,* followed closely by, *I'm going to kill Astara.* Gingerly pulling myself up, I swipe the back of my hand over my mouth, glaring at all four of them—including Leo, who looks like he is ready to bolt when our gazes connect. I am prepared to curse up a storm at all of them when the look on Fenrir's face stops me in the tracks.

"You were not sure if I'd be okay when I crossed through the portal." It's a statement, not a question, and a muscle jumps on the side of his jaw. "You fucking asshole!"

"You are perfectly fine." I'm not sure if he is trying to placate me or convince himself.

"That's beside the point." Snarling, I take a step towards him, balling my fists.

A loud crash followed by a crazed laugh jerks all our heads to the right. We are standing in a darkened alley, the light coming from the mouth of it barely reaching halfway through. Where we stand is devoid of everything, apart from a few ripped pages of a newspaper and some weird wrappers littering the ground. Puddles of murky water are spread in random places on the cracked pavement, and it leads to two large, metal containers near the front.

One of those containers is now bent in half, a significant dent in the middle of it making it look like it's trying to hug itself. A male is sprawled in front of it, groaning before he rolls on his hands and knees, shaking his head as if to clear it. It must be him denting the metal container in half, which tells me this is not a human. My fingers twitch to grab hold of the dagger I strapped to my thigh before coming here. Astara, who is standing closest to me, yanks me further back in the shadows, and I pull my eyes away from the male to see everyone has slunk deeper into the darkened alley to wait and see if we will be fighting it or letting it be.

"I'm going to kill you, bitch," the male snarls, lifting his head up just enough so the light illuminates his features.

My instincts kick up a notch when his skin flickers between the color of a human and a dark gray color. If that is not enough, his eyes turn red, leaving me with no doubt as to what he is: a demon. My foot lifts off the ground, every muscle relaxing so I can move, but I stay like that when a furl of movement enters the alley.

A woman, not really tall from what I can glimpse between her fast movements, hurls herself at the demon with a grin on her face. She is a tiny little thing, around my size but a foot or so shorter, with long pale locks streaming behind her. Two short swords are clutched in her hands, and I watch with my mouth hanging open as she hacks at the demon with abandon.

Two pained groans bounce off the dingy walls of the alley, and I know they come from Fenrir and Leo because I can feel Zoltan at my back where he moved to stand between his sister and me. The Fae and the shifter come out from where they were pressing their backs to the bricked wall, and glare at the woman. Something on Fenrir's face makes me do a double take, but the screams of the demon stop me from examining the Fae further.

"Wouldn't his screams bring the humans?" murmuring the question, I watch in fascination as the woman makes quick work of the snarling demon.

"No," the one-word wanderer from behind me says, explaining everything.

One of the short swords slides through the neck of the demon like through butter, a faint blue glow blinking so fast I would've missed it if I wasn't watching so closely. The headless body thumps on the ground, spraying the woman's legs with the murky water from the puddle at her knees. There is enough light where they are that I see her grimacing after jumping back away from it.

"These idiots owe me a new wardrobe by now." With a sigh, she walks up to the demon she decapitated and wipes her weapons off using his shirt. "That's why they should never send a man to do a woman's job."

None of us move, and I keep wondering what we are waiting for. The power coming off the woman is like a blast of hot air on my senses, alerting me to the threat that she is. Coiled up to fight, I hold my breath, my eyes not leaving her as she sheaths the swords at her back before turning our way, her hands on her hips.

"Look what the cat dragged in." She grins at Fenrir and Leo. It's a little unhinged, and I turn to see both males flinch. "You could've helped, you know." She flings a hand at the dead demon.

"Hello, Myst." Zoltan comes out from behind me, and I stiffen, expecting her to attack him.

"Hey, handsome." She winks, a real smile lifting her pouty lips.

My fangs drop from my gums, and I'm shocked to see I'm standing in front of Zoltan, baring them at her. Her smile grows.

"Take it easy there, chica." Lifting her hands in the air, Myst chuckles. "I'm not a fan of anyone chewing at my neck. He's all yours."

Fenrir grunts something intangible.

"Who are you?" My vicious snarl makes me wince, and she checks me out with a thoughtful frown.

"Alex was expecting you much sooner." Ignoring my question, she looks over my shoulder at Zoltan, tilting her head up to look him in the eye.

"We came as soon as we could. There are new developments we need to discuss." Zoltan turns me around by the shoulders, and after a moment, he moves around me, heading out of the alley.

Fenrir and Leo follow behind him, Myst falling in step with them. Astara comes next to me, and we both track them as they turn the corner and disappear in this new world I find myself in. All the stenches and sounds filter in and overwhelm my senses, so I breathe through my mouth in hopes of staying on my feet. Being here is like living a fantasy for me, yet I have a feeling I'll regret it sooner rather than later. If Daywalker Academy has taught me anything so far, it's that I should be cautious about what I wish for.

"You good?" Astara asks quietly from next to me.

"Who is that woman?" I like to think that it's jealousy rearing its ugly head, but I know better. Something about her is calling to me. It's as inviting as it is repelling.

"She is an acquaintance. One of the Fae we have helping us here."

"She didn't feel like Fae." Mumbling, I rub my arm, warding off a shiver that has nothing to do with being cold.

"Yeah, she's ... different, but Alex likes for us to keep our noses out of it. We need him, so we let it be for now." I can tell she's not happy being left out of the loop, and that soothes my worries somewhat.

"And Alex?"

"You'll see." Nudging me with her shoulder, she gets me moving closer to the street in front of us. "Where will the fun be if I tell you everything at once."

"This place makes me feel wild and not in control," I tell her truthfully. "It won't be fun if I attack someone I shouldn't."

"Trust me, if you attack this ass, I'll owe you a drink." Chuckling, she pulls me faster towards the mouth of the alley. "Let's go before my brother decides to come looking for us. I'm tired of his nagging."

I try very hard to chuckle at her joke, but it sounds strained. I have a bad feeling about all of this. A horrible, awful feeling.

Chapter Ten

By the time we reach a tall glass building, my neck develops a kink from straining to look at the top of it even though I'm unable to see anything but more glass, I'm agitated, hungry and angry. The damn humans can't drive to save their lives—nothing like in their movies. Lying little shits. The horn is the most used part of their rides, making me twitchy and giving Astara amusement to no end. The tip of my shoe bumps in a crack on the sidewalk, propelling me forwards as I stumble towards the sliding double doors in front of us.

"Careful, Miss." A young male dressed in a black suit grabs my upper arm, stopping me from faceplanting on the ground.

I flinch.

His scent hits me faster than a bolt of lightning. My head snaps in his direction and my mouth waters from the enticing smell of him. When our gazes connect, his chocolate-brown eyes widen a second before glazing over, and he tightens his hold on my arm. I watch him unblinking, unable to stop my fangs as they slide out of my gums.

I almost attack Astara when she yanks him away from me, forcing his head to twist away so he can look at her. "You were very tired, and you fell asleep on the job dreaming of a beautiful blonde woman coming to the building. You want to sleep now so you can dream of her, don't you?" she purrs in his ear, and I gape at her when he nods with a slack-jawed look on his face. "Go to sleep." She nudges him away gently, and he sways away from us as he stumbles inside the building.

"What the hell was that?" Straightening up, I roll my shoulders.

No amount of human television could've prepared me for this, and I've been here less than an hour. My eyes burn from all the flashing bright lights everywhere I turn. I have a pounding headache from the noise, and I'm trying very hard not to gag from the stench.

"Humans find it difficult to resist us." Astara smirks, pulling me along with her.

"I think it was a terrible idea for me to come here." I breathe through my mouth when we enter the building that is full of other humans. "You should've warned me their scent is so…" my words trail off because I can't find a word to describe what I feel. Enticing?

All-consuming is more like it.

No wonder we had the Purge.

Astara frowns slightly at me. "You get used to it." She sounds comforting but eyes me like she's expecting me to jump and slaughter them all. I don't blame her. They smell delicious.

They don't even glance at us as we pass the small clusters of people chatting among each other. A woman dressed in a shimmery dress bumps into me when she walks by, faltering slightly even though she continues on her way as if nothing happened. Turning my head, I search Astara's face and see the look of concentration on it.

"Just because you can screw with their minds doesn't mean you should." I don't know why her using her powers on them bothers me so much, but it does.

"Would you rather deal with drooling humans, Franky?" she says it so sweetly that I glare at her. "I didn't think so."

"I would've been fine if you weren't next to me." I stomp beside her in frustration. "I've never had anyone drooling over me, thank you very much."

"You've also not been around humans." Chortling, she points a finger in my face, and my eyes cross when I stare at her red nail. "And you are obviously blind if you think no one is drooling in Sienna. My brother included." When I try to grab her finger so I can break it, she snatches it away. "I think that's why I like you. You are clueless when it comes to how everyone perceives you."

"I'm not trying to attract a mate." Scowling at her, I stop in front of the silver doors of the elevator. "I'm half blood—"

Flinching, I grind my teeth when she slaps a hand over my mouth, silencing me. How I wish for the power to melt her with a look in this moment. Peeling her fingers off my face, I jut my jaw left and right to remove the strain her claw-like nails gives me.

"I'll be careful what I say while we are here." Turning away, she jabs the button on the wall.

"Why? They don't even see us thanks to your mind fuck." Folding my arms over my chest, I stare at the glowing numbers on top of the elevator doors.

"The humans are not the only ones in this building."

I keep my mouth shut when the elevator pings loudly and glides open, releasing a horde of humans at once. Jumping to the side so I don't get plowed through, I wait impatiently until we are both inside the mirrored walls, then the doors start closing. Taking a breath, I'm left with a slightly opened mouth when a hand shoves into the almost-closed doors, forcing them to open again. Astara stiffens next to me.

A male joins us, decked out in leather, his jacket straining over shoulders almost as wide as the doors. His light brown hair is short on the sides, and I can see the skin under it, though it is longer at the top of his head where it's sticking out every which way, like he's been running his fingers through it. Without a glance our way, he turns his back—which is an idiotic thing to do when you enter a tight space with two creatures that have fangs—and shoves a thick finger at one of the buttons. An aura of danger shrouds him like a cloak, and the monstrosity inside me perks up at that.

"Good to see you again, Astara." A voice so deep it sounds like rocks rolling down a hill makes me take a barely perceivable step back.

I see him smirk in the mirror without even looking at me, his square jaw cocking to the side.

"Who's your friend?"

I hold my breath for some reason.

"Zoltan is waiting for you. We just crossed over." Astara sounds like a soldier giving a report, staring straight ahead at her own reflection as she ignores his question.

It looks like I'm the only one confused here.

He turns over his shoulder to look at her, and I watch his profile as his gaze move up and down the length of Astara, a calculating look sparkling in his eyes. She stands as still as a statue, no emotion whatsoever on her face. The air thickens with tension, and my heartbeat slows. I have no idea who this asshole is, but if he so much as moves a finger in either of our directions, I'm going to paint the mirrors with his blood. His head swivels so fast my way it snaps me out of my trance-like state. Black eyes so dark I can't see his pupils lock on mine.

"Leave it be, Alex." Astara steps between us, breaking the staring match going on between us. "You need to talk to my brother."

"Yes." The elevator stops with a lurch, the doors sliding open with a loud ding, but he doesn't move. "I think we definitely need to talk."

My legs spread slightly as I place all my weight on the balls of my feet. I can still see his gaze over Astara's shoulder, although half of his face is hidden thanks to her head. He looks at me like I'm the strangest and most unexpected thing he's seen in his life. My skin prickles at the thought.

I don't like it.

I don't like it one little bit.

His arm shoots out, stopping the doors from closing without looking away from me. At this point, I'm getting more angry than worried about him acting like a dick, so grinding my teeth, I shoulder my way past both of them, ending up in a small little entrance area with just one round desk hugging the wall. Not a soul is around besides the three of us.

"Let's see what Zoltan has to say for himself." Alex, as Astara called him, steps out of the elevator, and she follows.

She comes next to me, linking her arm through mine as she drags me through the long hallway. I have to force myself not to look over my shoulder at Alex, who is walking behind us with a silent but measured gait. I can feel his eyes on me like they are the barrel of a gun pointing at the back of my head.

There is only one door in the entire floor and it takes us a few long minutes to reach. I'm guessing this is how it feels being forced to walk on a plank, with your heart in your throat and dread eating a hole in your stomach. In a rush, Astara opens the door and pulls me through it where I find myself the center of attention of a lot of pairs of eyes.

My gaze finds Zoltan's immediately.

Seeing his blue eyes bore into mine makes me realize just how tense I am until now. And how much having him around gives me a sense of safety I shouldn't have around anyone but myself. Roberti taught me that lesson not long ago.

"Zoltan." Alex jars me out of my thoughts.

Seeing Zoltan makes me forget about him completely. *You have a death wish, Franky*, I tell myself as both Astara and I pull away to find our place on either side of the vampire.

"Alex." Zoltan nods once, not bothering to unfold his arms that are straining his shirt within an inch of its life. "It took you long enough to get here."

"I had urgent matters. I can't be at your beck and call when it suits you." The deep, grumbly voice sounds casual, but the warning in it is evident. "I had to see Roberti regarding the breach in the portals."

Thankfully, Alex is walking towards a large wooden desk with his back to us when he says that. All of us stiffen at the mention of my old boss in a casual conversation after he tried to have all of us killed not a week ago. I find Myst watching me from the corner of the room, leaning shoulder on the wall behind her. I didn't even notice her standing there when I walked in. She gives me a slight shake of her head, and because I can't decide if it's a good or a bad thing, I look at Fenrir and Leo, who are as tight as springs standing next to a large floor-to-ceiling window. Alex plops onto the leather seat, making it protest under his weight, pulls my gaze back to him.

He is still watching me as if I'm the only person in the room.

"And what did Roberti say?" Zoltan leans forward in the chair he is sitting on, his words sucking all the oxygen in the room.

Finally, Alex looks at Zoltan, pursing his lips. The skin around his eyes scrunches up, his square jaw tightening. "He said it was a half blood. You wouldn't happen to know anything about that, would you?" His eyes flick to me then back to Zoltan pointedly.

"Ms. Drake is a student at the academy." Fenrir pushes off the large window and straightens. "I would worry about who you keep around yourself more than who we take in our ranks, Alexius."

I can feel Myst bristle from across the room. The moment we saw her in that alley, Fenrir's knickers were in a knot, and they still are, but right now isn't the time to worry about it. By the way the males are talking to each other, and at the mention of Roberti, I have a feeling shit is about to hit the fan. The tension is so thick that when Alex sighs and relaxes his shoulders, it's like a bubble popping in my ears allowing us to breathe.

"Alright, alright." Lifting palms as large as my head in surrender, Alex chuckles, the aggression in the air disappearing so suddenly my knees almost buckle. "I figured it was a bullshit story as soon as he called to meet up. The mighty Roberti asking me to see him is not something I will pass up, something I think you know." He grins at Zoltan.

This fucker must be really old to have that much power.

"He had a lot to say about your *Ms. Drake*." Leaning thick forearms on the desk, Alex laces his fingers. "He was trying very hard to make me see the danger she represents for all of us. Too hard, you see. Enough for me to smell bullshit. So, what gives?"

"You better not be working with him," Zoltan says softly, but the hairs on my arms lift from the punch of power coming from him. "I will personally end your life very slowly if that's the case."

"I wouldn't have lived this long if I didn't know how to pick the winning side, my friend."

"The academy has been infiltrated. We have someone on the inside working against us. They started killing through the streets of Sienna, and now they are killing inside our walls. Your friend Roberti is neck deep in this." Zoltan's fingers tighten slightly on the armrests of the chair, the only indication of his anger. "They are trying to bring the portals down."

Alex jerks back and his mouth opens as if to speak, but he doesn't get the chance. A loud boom makes the building shudder, and we stumble slightly, trying to keep our balance. Alex jumps off his chair, looming over the desk.

"You brought hunters to my doors!" he roars at Zoltan, and that is the last straw for me. I can't take anymore shit and I certainly am done being quiet.

"That's your buddy Roberti sending a 'you are a dumbass' thank-you card, asshole." Snarling at him, I spin around, leaping at the door and yanking it open.

I might not have dealt with human hunters in my life, but I stand a better chance of fighting a living being than being buried under a ton of slabs from a collapsed building.

Chapter Eleven

Adrenaline pumps through my veins as I reach the elevator doors. The building shudders again, pushing the urgency I feel to a whole new level. I breathe through my nose harshly, hoping to keep the magic inside me at bay—at least until I know what I'm dealing with. Seeing a door to the right with an exit sign on it, I jerk it open and enter a dark, empty space with stairs leading up and down but nothing else. When the door clicks closed behind me, a bright light flicks automatically on, blinding me for a moment.

Flinching with a hiss, I shield my eyes, pressing my back to the wall and hoping no one else has thought of using the stairs or I might be screwed. Ever since the night I became bound to the academy, I feel like I haven't been myself. My usual knee jerk reactions that get me out of clusterfucks like this are nowhere to be found, and I'll end up dead if I don't snap out of it.

When the bright spots disappear and my vision clears, two things become crystal clear. One: there is no one using the stairs, not that I can hear at the moment anyway. Two:

whatever that sound and shuddering are, they are definitely not a physical attack on this building. Awareness of Zoltan comes soon after, telling me he is getting very close. Glancing over my shoulder like a frightened deer, my body leans forward, ready to bolt down the stairs. I take one step and stop dead in my tracks, my head snapping back to look at the door. A thin layer of white powder lines the frame. Tracing it with my gaze, I see it on the ground as well, so I kneel to get a better look.

With a slight flick, I dust off the floor, rubbing the powder gently between my fingers. The small grains roll under the pressure of my skin, and I bring it under my nose, sniffing cautiously. Unable to pinpoint the scent, I bring it to the tip of my tongue, aware that if it's a poison that can affect supernaturals, I deserve to die for doing something so stupid. The moment the tiny grain touches my taste buds, I frown.

Salt.

I leap back, grabbing the metal railing at my back when the door opens suddenly. Zoltan fills up the frame, looming like Death himself has come to claim me. His eyes lock on my still-clutched fingers before flicking back to my face.

"It wards off demonic forces." Not moving away from the threshold, he searches my face.

"What does that mean?" My fingers rub together absentmindedly. "Demons can't enter the stairs? I feel safer already," I add dryly, wondering who has come up with this idiotic idea.

His lips quirk at the corners, but the intense gaze he throws my way keeps me pinned to the spot. I clutch the railing tighter, the metal bending in my grasp. The ping from the elevator door sounds from somewhere behind him, but Zoltan doesn't even twitch a muscle.

"Remember how I said the gifts from the old gods change the hunters?" At my reluctant nod, his eyebrow lifts up in an arch. "The salt is a millennium-known protection from evil spirits, so they can't cross the warding unless the line is broken."

My heart jumps in my throat, and my eyes lock on the ground under Zoltan's boots, where I dusted off the line of salt. "Umm, I actually…" my words trail off.

"There is one more protection set around the building." He turns to look at something over his shoulder for a moment before pinning me with a narrowed look. "Unless someone broke that one as well, they'll stay outside of it."

Another boom makes me sway, my tight grip on the metal the only thing preventing me from toppling down the stairs. Zoltan is next to me faster than a bolt of lightning, anchoring me to his body with an arm around my waist. My knees almost buckle, his nearness making me dizzy, and I lean towards him, pressing closer. A barely audible groan vibrates in his chest, and my head snaps up so I can see his face.

When I tip my face up, Zoltan's lips are so close to mine I can feel the air heating where our skin almost touches, but a breath away. The strength of his grip molds the very hard muscle of his body to mine, and I feel his erection burning a hole in my lower belly. Butterflies are wreaking havoc in my stomach, and his eyes lock on the fluttering pulse on my neck. A deaf person can hear the thundering in my chest, and the metal in my hand screeches painfully loud when it snaps in half, biting into my palm.

"I'll start thinking I'm making the famous Agent Drake nervous," he murmurs, his pillowy lower lip grazing mine with each word. The familiar smirk on his face speeds up my breathing, but something nags at me deep down, pummeling my head insistently.

My mouth tingles.

"I want to stab something." Blurting out the first thing I can think of, I watch him frown.

"You what?" I almost laugh at the incredulous look on his handsome face.

"I want to stab something." Leaning closer to him, my cheek brushes his when I whisper in his ear. I can feel him shiver slightly, and I want to hoot with pride for making him react that way. "So, either point the way to where I can see these hunters that all of you are talking about or be ready to fight me. But don't you ever again try to sidetrack me by using my attraction to you, Zoltan." He leans back with a shocked look, and this time I smirk at him. "You won't like what happens if you do."

"I don't think it's wise for the hunters to get a whiff of you, Francesca." A muscle jumps in his jaw. "Not yet."

"You know it would've been easier to say that instead of trying to manipulate me." I nudge him, and his hold on me loosens, allowing me to slip away from his grasp. "If they are here, it means they know something. And if anyone knows me better than I know myself, that would be Roberti. He would've expected me to come and see for myself the moment I found out about everything."

"More the reason for you to stay away from this fight." He stops me with a grip on my arm when I try to step down the stairs down. "There will be other fights. Let us keep them in the dark as long as we can."

"And leave the others to fight on their own?" Yanking my arm away, I take the stairs two at a time with him hot on my heels. "Not a chance, pure blood. You can sit and watch if you like. I'm going to kick some human ass right about now."

The walls blur as I move as fast as I can, holding the railing to stop myself from bouncing off them. The gray color of the paint mixes with the white of the tiles and the glare of the light, giving me a headache. The lower we get, the harder my stomach lurches. The only thing stopping me from leaning over and hurling is knowing that the arrogant vampire is right behind me.

My skin prickles, the tiny hairs standing on end when both my feet hit the ground level. I can feel Zoltan slowing down as well, his presence as comforting at my back as it is annoying. I'm still not sure how I feel after his little charade up there.

"Let us be smart about this, Francesca." His massive hand slams on the door, thwarting my attempt to open it. "If there is no need for you to get involved, stay out of it and just observe. That's all I ask."

Giddiness and anticipation swirl inside me. I'm debating if slapping Zoltan will move him out of my way faster, or if it'll turn into us fighting each other in this claustrophobic space. Nodding with a jerk is enough to get him to step away, and a blast of cold air hits my face when I yank the heavy door open. I may be a little over enthusiastic since I almost rip it off the hinges, but with a sheepish side glance, I step into the lobby.

Right into a war zone.

Jumping back, stepping on Zoltan's toes in the process, I avoid an arrow whose steel tip embeds itself in the door-frame, missing both of us by only an inch.

It's chaos.

I spot our four companions easily, all of them in head-to-toe black, making them stand out between a dozen or more white as snow ninjas. The scene if front of my eyes is so insane that the thought makes me snort, but it's the only word my mind can connect with the so-called hunters—if these are even the hunters I was told about.

Zoltan pulls me to the side, slipping behind a large wooden screen separating the open lobby of the building from a short hallway. At a closer look, I realize the two doors are the bathrooms, and I receive a glare from Zoltan for my snickering. A Daywalker and a half blood walk into the bathroom ... there is a joke there somewhere, I just can't think of it at the moment.

A shift in the temperature and the stirring in the air triggers the monstrous magic inside me, and I jerk my head back. Another arrow sinks through the thin screen where my head used to be. I can feel its vibrations on the tip of my nose from the nonexistent proximity to it. Anger surges through me. The fuckers will nail me to a wall while I hide like a coward.

"How are the humans not reporting this?" Voicing what bothers me, I crawl closer to the corner, ignoring the fact that my ass is stuck in Zoltan's face. Well, I try to ignore it, but it's there in the back of my mind trying to send all sorts of inappropriate images in my mind. *Now is not the time, Franky. Plus, he is a manipulative jerk, remember?* the voice in my head adds its two cents shaking me out of it.

"Fenrir will not allow them to see it." Zoltan sounds pained from behind me, and I bite my lip hard so I don't laugh. The pants I'm wearing are molded to my ass so I can imagine the view he has. "The hunters know that. We have a lot more to lose if all of them know about our existence."

I forget all about humans and if they can see us when I stick my head around the corner. The number of hunters has doubled, cornering our friends, making me think they will never get out of there alive. Except that weird chick from earlier and Alex stand in different spots, separating them from each other in the vast space. It takes me a moment to see what is actually going on. Even though weapons are being shot or thrown their way, they are not getting hurt. Moving faster than the hunters, they twist and turn, avoiding anything that might harm them. Yet, they are being hoarded away from the area me and Zoltan are occupying. While I watch, a handful of the white-dressed hunters peel off from the rest, slinking in the background and heading our way. My heart picks up a beat.

I grin.

"Zoltan?" Not taking my eyes away from them, my mind is spinning with ideas that the vampire behind me is going to hate. My grin widens.

"No," he hisses, not wanting to even hear what I have to say.

"Let's say I stay back and observe this fight so I can familiarize myself with the hunters." Ignoring his naysay attitude, I keep eyeing the hunters that are getting closer.

"You'll stay back and observe, there is no, 'let's say' about it." Grumbling behind me, he wiggles behind me in attempt to get a better look. The moment he is level with me, his body stiffens, and my smile hurts my cheeks.

"But if they bring the fight to me ..." my words trail off when my eyes lock on hazel ones.

The hunter freezes, his eyes widening slightly before narrowing into slits. I've seen hatred many times. I've been hunting criminals and whack jobs most of my life through the streets of Sienna. I've never seen evil like the one staring me in the face right now. There is nothing humane in this human hunter. Like black holes that will swallow everything around them, those eyes darken the longer I keep looking at them.

"Jack," Zoltan says from next to me, and it breaks the connection between the hunter and me.

I shiver, pulling back for a moment. Unless there is something in the air making me hallucinate, I could swear his face is morphing in front of my eyes. The smooth skin visible from the facemask covering the lower part of his face is wrinkling and bunching up, turning leathery and definitely not human.

"You know one of them?" I'm hoping a conversation can shake off this uneasy feeling running through me.

"We need to get you out of here." Ignoring my question, Zoltan stands up, lifting me along with him. "We can go to the roof. If they need to come up, it'll be easier to hold them back."

I'm listening to him speak, but I do not hear a word. Something inside me wants to face that creature disguised as a human and teach him a lesson. A new heartbeat starts inside my chest, getting louder the longer I think about it. My senses stretch out, reaching for something that shouldn't be in this world of humans, and the moment I feel the hunter near, my energy recoils from it. My heart slows down to barely a beat. The hunter is so close I can hear him breathing. Zoltan clenches his jaw, his eyes flashing bright blue, the pupils expanding like small suns. No time for running up the stairs because the fight found its way to me. The calm washes over me and my vision changes, bringing every microscopic detail into focus.

Thump.

Chapter Twelve

My hand shoots out, twisting in Zoltan's shirt and yanking him back. My back bows, the end of my braid curling on the floor behind me, and I feel the stirring of air on my chest from the long sword piercing the wall. The vibrating blade is pulled out, disappearing from view, and I straighten, releasing my hold on the vampire. I shove him to the side and his back hits the opposite wall while my foot kicks out, hitting the blade stabbing through the wall again. The steel bends but it doesn't break, the tip stopping between Zoltan's hands only an inch from his chest.

The Daywalker holds the sharp sword between his palms for a breath before he steps aside, twists around, and wrenches it through the drywall. Plaster explodes in a cloud of dust and debris, letting the deadly weapon clutter to the ground.

Thump.

A fist punches through the same wall, making the hole bigger. The clenched hand is large and scarred with ripped, bloody knuckles caked with grit and grime. Black swirls crawl up the forearm, but I have no interest in looking at them. Taking hold of the wrist with both hands and planting both feet firmly on the floor, I tug it as hard as I can, snapping the arm at the elbow. The cracking of the bone breaking sets my teeth on edge. The arm bends at the wrong angle and the deafening scream is like music to my ears.

Zoltan pounces, pushing off the floor with so much strength his body passes through the drywall like he jumps through an open window as he disappears from my sight. Not wanting to be left behind, I jump through the hole, too, landing on the other side right next to him. We are both facing a pissed-off hunter cradling his broken arm to his chest. The hunter stares icily at me, snapping his bone back in place with a sickening crunch. I don't have time to wonder how he heals so fast when he throws his body at Zoltan, his fist is aimed at my head.

I watch him move in slow motion.

His feet push off the ground, the muscles of his thighs flexing in the tight clothing he wears and propelling him forward. I see the fingers of his left hand curling up, reaching for the tip of a dagger sticking out from under his sleeve. He aims it at Zoltan's chest while his right fist moves in an arch, coming directly at my face. Bending my knees, I crouch down and slide under the hunter's body before I pull my arm back like a sling shot, shooting my flat palm up into his chest. My hips twist, the power of the hit coming from my lower body and giving it more strength than is necessary, resulting in a shattered ribcage.

Thump.

The hunter drops dead at my feet, blood trickling from his lips and pooling under him from his chest. I grin at Zoltan, but he is not looking at me. His glower is aimed at something in front of us, so I follow his line of sight. The evil one is still alive—the one with the shifting face—standing behind a wall of hunters surrounding us in half circle. The dead hunter at my feet is just a random, unfortunate soul who must think it is a fun idea to pick a fight with freaks like me.

Metal flips through the air, a curtain of shuriken, the deadly throwing stars are coming at us from all sides and cutting the space with laser precision. My heart kicks up a beat, harshly lurching a *thump, thump* too loud for my ears. I can see the metal stars splitting the air slowly, but they might be too fast for the Daywalker next to me. When the first one gets near, I slap it aside from him, embedding it in the wall behind us. To my surprise, Zoltan does the same, covering my back and moving as fast as I am. Stepping back-to-back, we start moving in an orchestrated dance, punching, kicking, twisting, and whirling.

Thump.

Sidestepping Zoltan, I kick my foot over my head, bringing my upper body low to the floor as I sweep one of the stray shurikens. When I raise up, I flick it at the hunter who had my full attention from the start. Before he has time to move, the star sinks into his shoulder, painting his white clothing red. At the sight of his blood, my fangs drop.

Zoltan tenses but doesn't stop moving, his body twisting and turning like a contortionist on crack. The faster the attacks come, the more natural his movements—and the more accurate for that matter. Four of the hunters surrounding us are already littering the ground at his feet. I'm still on just one, staring at him instead of cleaning up the trash adamant to kill me. When a dagger is thrown my way again, I lurch forward, tuck my shoulder in, and roll, ending up right in front of the one I want to kill more than the rest. Maybe their idea was to separate me from the Daywalker, but I have the evil one in my grasp now. Seeing him face to face awakens something inside me.

An all-consuming darkness starving for life.

The hunter's eyes widen, the hatred on his face being replaced with terror unlike anything I've ever seen on another opponent. It startles me out of my trance-like state, and as we stand staring at each other like death isn't having a feast between these walls tonight, the bitter, sour stench of the blood streaming down his shoulder insults my senses. My nostrils flare from the offending odor, and my fangs throb in my gums, urging me to rip his throat out right here and now.

I grin at his fear-stricken face, the tips of my fangs pushing my upper lip above them. The corner of his left eye twitches slightly, the muscle jumping and pulling his eyelid down. His shoulders tense, telling me he is about to move, and my own body stiffens in readiness to fight. I move fast—faster than his human senses can register no matter who he sold his soul to. My fingers wrap around the cloth covering his features below his eyes and I yank it off him so I can see the face of the man wanting to kill me simply because I'm different than him.

Searing pain in my right arm rips a scream from my throat, and the hunter uses the distraction to turn and run. Fucking coward. Something barrels into me, sending me rolling on the floor, my mouth filling with the coppery taste of my own blood when my face hits the tiles, causing my fangs to pierce the inside of my lip. Snarling, I plant both palms flat of the ground and push as hard as I can to get whoever it is off me. A yelp is followed by a vicious growl when I spin around crouched and ready to pounce. My eyes connect to intelligent green eyes I'm familiar with, only I've never seen them on a furry face before now.

Leo.

My head swivels left and right as I search for immediate threats, but I only find the lobby of the building littered with dead hunters, those that survived on the heels of my running-away nemesis. Fingers curling, my nails bite into the hard, unforgiving tiles when my gaze locks on the hunter's, who is standing partially out of the front doors. His buddies are leaving as fast as their legs can carry them, while he just stands there watching me as if he is trying to memorize my face.

Spitting to the side, I bare my bloody teeth in the mockery of a smile. Unknown to him, this fucker gives me what I am missing—and had been ever since the murders started in Sienna. I had nothing tangible to fight against. I was chasing shadows with no direction and had no idea what I was looking for.

I was running blind. Now I'm not.

I didn't miss the swirls of shadows in his gaze when we stood in front of each other. That darkness was answered by my own.

In this moment, I learn his face so I can remember it. It seers into my retinas, his soulless eyes and disfigured features. My smile shows him the promise I just made to myself. I'm going to hunt him down. I will enjoy every single second of it.

And he will die.

He has become my target, and his nod before he disappears through the doors tells me I am his, too. He accepts my challenge, and now the game is on. My breathing speeds up, adrenaline rushing through my veins and making me feel lightheaded with excitement.

Hissing when a muzzle bumps into my arm that still burns from whatever hurt me, I turn to look at Leo. The wolf is much larger than I anticipated, no doubt standing as tall as I am if he lifts on his hind legs. His massive head blocks my view, those eyes making sure I'm paying attention. My eyes cross when I notice a white spot on his nose in hopes of seeing it better.

And then the fucker licks my face.

"You disgusting mongrel!" Scrunching my nose, I shove him away, wiping the back of my good arm over the slime dripping from my nose and chin.

Leo curls his upper lip in a snarl over elongated canines as long as my pinky. A shiver dances up my spine from the feral look on his face. The dark fur bristles as his growl becomes louder. I don't understand his behavior until I'm yanked by the arm, a pathetic half moan/half scream coming out of my mouth.

"Can you walk, or should I carry you?" Fenrir's pretty face comes into view when my eyes stop rolling to the back of my head from the pain. A strand of his long blond hair falls over one eye.

"Not ewy female whys to be swept off her feet by a pwetty boy, Fae." My words are slurred, and I'm freaking out inside my head. I have no control over what I'm saying. "What the … fuc … is goin' on?"

"They used potions on their weapons," Fenrir growls, fighting my flailing arms while I'm trying to stop him from picking me up. "We need to get you to a mage before you lose your mind."

My heart jumps in my throat, panic squeezing me like a vise and preventing my lungs from inflating. What the hell does he mean I'll lose my mind? Is this thing permanent? And why did no one warn me? *It's not like you would've listened to them if they did,* the voice in my head chirps, pissing me off.

"Zoltan … Astara?" I'm reduced to one-word sentences now. At least I'm winning in the drunken fight to keep the Fae away. Yay, me!

"They are fine." When he huffs, I snicker, causing him to step away and plant his fists on his hips. My flailing wins against the royal Fae. "It's better they stay away from you while you're bleeding. Keeping Alex away is a brilliant idea, too."

"I don't like him."

When I pout at that, I realize I'm in more trouble than I originally thought. My tongue is tingling, the colors around me getting brighter with each blink. My eyes dart around, landing on a dagger near the wolf's paws. It's made of black steel with some white markings on it, but what gets my attention is the few tiny drops of a black substance under it. I point at it mutely with a shaking finger, and Fenrir seizes it with a worried look on his face.

"We can't carry you through the wards and the portal like this. We need to get to a mage here." Turning to Leo, Zoltan nods, and the wolf loops his large body to stretch over the dead bodies of the hunters.

"It still smells like a wet doggy in here." Wrinkling my nose, I rub at it with the back of my hand.

"Don't let him hear you say that." Snorting, the Fae grins when the feral growl bounces off the vaulted ceilings of the lobby.

"I'm going to kill him, you know." Numbness starts spreading through my body, and I sway on my feet.

"Leo?" The Fae frowns at me.

My knees give out, and I start going down, but luckily, Fenrir is there to scoop me up before I hit the ground. In his rush to grab me, one of his hands slides under the hem of my shirt, giving me skin to skin contact. The fear that he hides so well hits me like a punch to the sternum, taking my breath away. I stare at his too-perfect face as he cradles me to his chest like a child.

"No, the hunter." I search his face, but he won't look at me, pulling his hand away to place it over the fabric of my shirt. "If I live." His arms tighten at that. "Am I going to die from one scratch, Fae?"

"Not if I can help it, Francesca." He finally turns his head and locks his gaze on mine. "No one dies on my watch, least of all, you."

His eyes transform into the black ones with a white pupil, letting me see the real him and the determination there to do everything he can to keep me breathing. Bobbing my head up and down slowly, I lean it on his shoulder as he starts walking out of the place. My lids are getting heavy, numbness and fear for Zoltan and Astara swirling inside me like a tornado, and I have to press my lips tight so I don't empty my stomach all over myself and Fenrir's shirt.

I have no doubt in my mind that Fenrir will do everything in his power to help me get better. Whether he finds help on time, well that's a totally different matter. That hunter today earned himself a place on the top of my list of people to kill. After this—if I live—I'm not just going to hunt him down and kill him.

I'm going to kill everything around him, and everyone he holds dear.

When the fresh air hits my face, Fenrir's even gait lulls me further into closing my eyes, but I manage to look over his shoulder at the building we are leaving behind. I can feel Leo next to us still in his wolf form, his panting even and calm, the coarse hairs of his fur brushing against the back of my limp arm. Flames lick the outside walls of the tall tower, reaching to the second floor. Sound from the real world returns in a rush, shrill sirens overtaking the screams and yells of humans trying to see what is going on. The rush of activity is but a blur of colors forcing my eyes fully closed.

"Destroy the evidence," murmuring under my breath, I have no idea why I find this situation and that particular statement so important, but I succumb to the poison before I figure it out.

Chapter Thirteen

I can feel my clothing sticking to my skin like I've been doused with a bucket of water. The heat is unbearable, causing sweat to trickle under my hair and down my neck. My head is thrashing on a drenched pillow, and I fight my way out of whatever is preventing me from opening my eyes to no avail. Even the magic that has its claws sank deeply in me is quiet. That's one thing that should worry me, but the frustration of not being able to see where I am and what's going on is stronger, pushing it aside.

"She's reacting to it," A male voice says in frustration as if I'm putting him off by merely being alive.

"I don't need her to react; I need her to wake up." Hearing Fenrir stops my thrashing.

"She is not even supposed to be here, so stop acting like all this is my fault," the male snaps at Fenrir and the heat making me want to peel my skin off so I can cool down doubles.

Where am I? the question screams in my head while I gulp freezing air that bypasses my throat and settles in my lungs. The heat and cold pummel me inside with such opposing forces that my mouth opens wider on a silent scream.

Not a sound comes out.

"Zoltan will be here any minute. If you value your life, I'd make sure she's awake by then." Footsteps move away from me; a moment later, Fenrir hisses, and the scent of blood spreads around me like moon rays after a cloudy night. My mouth waters as I turn my face towards the smell on instinct alone.

"I'm not sure that will help," the male drawls.

"It can't hurt either."

Fenrir's voice gets louder as he nears, the bed dipping when he settles his weight on it. A hand pushes under my head, the fingers tangling in the wet strands of my hair when he lifts me up. When a warm glass is pressed to my lips, I part them eagerly, letting the thick blood slide down my parched throat. It's fresh and compelling, the essence of it confirming it's the Fae feeding me his own lifeforce after bleeding in a cup.

Drinking it greedily, I can't help but wonder why the Fae is being so protective of me. Not just after Soren screwed me over by tying my life to what keeps them all what they are. Even before that, Fenrir was circling around like a shark who smelled fresh blood. I'm sure it's not attraction. It might've been at first, way back when he and Zoltan were beating their fists over their chest like gorillas over a bitch in heat. But he accepted that I didn't see him in that light with grace. So, what makes him hover over me like a mother hen, dealing with my crappy attitude with a trembling hand?

I lose my train of thought when he lifts the glass higher than necessary, filling my mouth with more blood than I can swallow. It trickles down the sides of my face, and I tilt my chin up with tightly pressed lips pushing the cup away before choking on the large gulp and almost coughing out a lung. My chest burns while I curl up on my side, hacking, my arms wrapping around my middle.

"She should be fully awake now." The male's voice sounds breathy, like he's been running a marathon.

"Francesca, can you hear me?" Fenrir pushes the hair off my face, his large palm settling on my back and rubbing it gently. "You don't have to speak, just open your eyes."

"There are easier ways to kill me, you know," I rasp, still choking with my eyes pressed tightly shut.

"Yes, we almost figured that out." The Fae chuckles weakly, the relief in his voice pulling my eyelids open.

His hand stops the small circles he is petting on my back when my gaze locks on his. I see the blood drain from his face through blurry, stinging eyes—probably from the coughing fit I'm trying to keep at bay. Confused, I move my face to see who else is in the room, but my cheek sticks to the drenched fabric of the sheet under my head, making it more difficult. Finally, I'm able to turn, and the moment I lock eyes with a male sitting on a chair next to the bed, he howls something and jumps away from me, toppling over the falling chair.

"Fates, help us." Crab walking away from the bed I'm curled on, he lifts one hand, making some sort of signs in the air. "What have you done?"

"If you don't stop whatever it is you're doing, I'm going to drain you dry." My throat feels raw like I've been chewing on shards, and I frown at the male.

"Breathe, Francesca. Close your eyes and deep breaths," Fenrir butts in, pulling my focus away from the weirdo still waving his hand in my face.

"You were just begging me to open them." Hissing at him through clenched teeth, I'm reminded again of how he pales when I look at him. "Shit. It's my eyes, isn't it? They are ..." Closing them tight, I breathe through my nose.

Damn snake eyes. Well, dragon eyes, now that I know what creature is mixed in my DNA. I never heard of it before I stupidly went to the academy. I still know next to nothing about it, either, only that I scare the shit out of everyone—like I didn't do that before my eyes started going all freaky ... Just one more thing that makes Francesca Drake an abomination.

When clothing ruffles and the air changes around me, I lift my lids slightly, seeing Fenrir stand up. In one step, he is in front of the male still sitting on the floor, yanking him up by the hand that is making those weird signs. He mumbles something intangible under his breath, and with a shocked look painting his face, he looks up at the Fae. The same second his eyes glaze over and a slack smile lifts the corners of his lips. I fully open my eyes, watching them both. Fenrir whispers something I can't hear from the rushing of blood through my veins, and the male turns around, leaving the room with a soft click of the door closing behind him.

"I thought vamps were the only ones that could screw with your mind." Lifting on my elbows, I squint at the Fae.

"I've learned a trick or two throughout the years." He gives me a lopsided smile that doesn't reach his eyes.

"Through the centuries, you mean?"

"Or that." With a slight nod, he turns to face me fully. "How do you feel?"

Searching inside myself, I consider his question. "I don't feel like I'm about to burst into flames if that's what you're asking." My mouth twists in a grimace, and I pluck the wet shirt gingerly on my chest between two fingers. "At least I'm alive, right?"

"There was never a danger to your life per se." He dismisses my questioning look with a wave of his hand, his long fingers flicking the air. "There was a danger to your life as you know it. The hunters use potions that change who we are inside."

Swinging my legs to the side, I sit up on the edge of the bed, forgetting all about the discomfort of my sweaty clothes or the wet hair plastered to my head and face. My breathing speeds up, uneasiness gnawing a hole in my stomach. The feeling of my body going numb and shutting down returns with a vengeance, reminding me how powerless it feels to be unable to fight it. I thought it was killing me.

I guess that makes me wrong.

"What does that mean?" Fenrir starts pacing at my question, his long legs doing a three-step walk back and forth in front of me.

"We think …" A, long graceful finger is shoved in my face. "We don't know for sure, so don't go jumping to conclusions. This is all a speculation so far." He waits for my nod before blowing out a harsh breath out. "They either have a mighty mage on their side with magic as ancient as the one the Board has, or …"

I wait while he frowns at his moving feet, glaring at them as if they hold all the knowledge he wants as hostage. With the mention of old magic, I look within, hoping to feel the monster inside me stir, but it doesn't. Since my legs can't hold me up, it manages to somehow retreat and hide from me. Trying to be rid of it for so long now, I never think I will actually miss feeling it.

Fenrir sucks in a lungful of air, pulling me from my

head. "Or, they are using the blood from one of the old gods." He whirls on me so fast I find myself sprawled across the bed. "And before you say it, I know how insane that sounds. It's unheard of, preposterous even."

"Fenrir ..." I sit up again.

"No one in their right mind will go anywhere near to draw blood from one of the old ones. I know it; Zoltan knows it." His arms are now waving around angrily, chopping through the air. "Even a moronic creature would know it, just by survival instinct alone."

"Fenrir!" shouting his name stops his meltdown into insanity. "I get it, okay? Calm down." I go for a placating smile, but by the look on his face, I probably look constipated. "No one in their right mind would go near them. Got it. So, what type of a mage can pull shit like this? And you still haven't told me what exactly it does, this potion."

"It turns any supernatural feral." He clenches his jaw tightly, and I can hear his teeth grinding. "If it's not caught and pushed out of the bloodstream in time, it can turn any of us into a beast—a monster. I've seen it happen too many times."

My heart stops, my stomach dropping to my feet. Snapping my head to the side, I claw at my shirt, ripping the sleeve at the seams and tossing it away from me. A tingling in my skull warns me that it's not natural to react like this after the fact, but I can't stop my nails scraping at the skin where the cut used to be. Red welts form where I keep scratching at it until a chilly, calloused hand grips them, stopping me from making myself bleed. I look up at Zoltan's handsome face.

I didn't feel or hear him coming.

"We can't be sure it's all out." My words come in a rush, all the breath exiting my lungs at once. Fenrir sticks his head over the vampire's shoulder, watching me with too-wide eyes.

Not taking his eyes off me, Zoltan lifts my hand to his mouth. One of his nails transforms into a black, sharp talon that pierces my wrist. Still watching me, his soft lips press on my skin, and I feel the pull all the way to my lower belly when he takes a mouthful of my blood. A low groan deep in his throat lifts the short hairs on my neck. His look is so intimidating and terrifying that my heartbeat picks up a notch, hammering my ribcage.

His tongue licks a small circle there, pebbling my skin, his pupils shrinking and dilating a few times while I hold my breath. The air is charged with something so intense it almost makes me want to crawl under his skin and never get out from under. My fists clench to stop me from moving.

Fenrir clears his throat uncomfortably.

"Your blood is your own." Zoltan's deep voice sends a tremor through me, and I shiver.

"Good to know." I clear my throat twice before I'm able to reply, and I tug gently on my arm, silently asking him to release me. "You didn't answer my second question." I glance at the Fae over Zoltan's shoulder.

"Right," Fenrir straightens, tugging on the bottom of his shirt that somehow ended up untucked from his pants. I frown at it. "It must be a powerful mage, a very old one at that."

"How old?" Something nags at me in the back of my mind, getting more slippery the harder I try to grasp it. "Soren old, or you old?"

"Me old would do the trick, I suppose." His eyebrows pull low over his eyes.

"So, we are talking about ancient fucks here, huh?" My attempt to lighten the situation goes down the drain when he glares at me. "You don't have a sense of humor, Fae. Otherwise, I'm hilarious."

Jerking back, I scowl at Zoltan when he sniffs in my direction. "I'm sweaty, I know. I nearly went feral on you two, remember? No need to be rude."

"You fed her your blood." Ignoring me, Zoltan whirls on Fenrir like he carries the wrath of God in his soul.

"I had to bleed her while the mage worked. I saved her life." Lifting his chin in defiance, the Fae stares down his nose at the slightly taller vampire. It's impressive to watch, really. Then his words hit me.

"You did what?" Screeching, I jump off the bed. The fucker didn't just say he was bleeding me while I was unconscious.

Something stirs in my chest, and the thought of the magic inside me waking up sniffles my anger for a moment. I press the palm of my hand between my breasts, willing it to show me it's still there. Somewhere along the way, the feeling that I need it as much as I need air cemented itself in my head.

"Astara is missing."

Zoltan drops the mother of all bombs, and I plop back on the bed.

Chapter Fourteen

"She was right behind me when we chased them through the city," Zoltan growls through his teeth. "She separated from me for just a block and never showed up after that."

"This is not the first time she's fought hunters. She knows better than to get herself trapped." Fenrir sounds like he is trying to convince himself, not Zoltan.

"I don't understand why we are still talking?" My fists keep clenching and unclenching on my thighs. "Let's go find her."

"I'm sure she would love knowing that you care about her enough to go looking, but I think we should just wait." Folding his arms over his chest, Zoltan sighs, leaning back on the wall. "This is not the first time she has gone off on her own when it comes to them."

"You didn't sound very excited about her disappearing in the middle of a chase when you told us." Frustration eats at me when he just stares at me blankly. "I was here when you said it. Astara is missing." Mimicking his deep voice, I manage to get him to glower at me harder.

"We wait." There is finality in his words, making them sound like an order, and anger rears its head inside me. Fenrir nods sharply like an excellent little soldier.

"You're not the boss of me." Internally, I flinch at how stupid that sounds, but I'll be damned if I let them see it. Zoltan's eyebrows climb all the way to his hairline.

"You are not going anywhere near the hunters, Ms. Drake." His low words are like stroked coals starting a fire inside me. I'm back to Ms. Drake now, too. "You are too weak after being injured."

"How dare you, you motherfucker." Snarling, I can feel my eyes shifting when every detail of his face becomes crystal clear, including the veins under his skin. "If you told me what I could be facing, I wouldn't have been in a position to get injured."

The trademark smirk returns to his face.

It's panty melting to be sure, and it makes my knees weak even now, but I'm too pissed off to let it destruct me. His face is so intense, I can feel cold sweat beading on my upper lip. The magic makes a pathetic attempt at stirring up, but it evaporates as fast as it comes. Poor Fenrir looks like he wants to crawl into a tiny hole and hide. At least he keeps his mouth shut.

"And what would you have done differently if you were told?" This Zoltan reminds me of the asshole I first met, arrogant and just a plain old jerk.

"Not saved your ass when they wanted to skewer you, for starters." Gloating at his glower, I cross my own arms. "I would've paid closer attention to their weapons instead of everything else."

"You should always pay the most attention to the weapons, regardless of how harmless you think they are." Pushing off the wall, he looms over me, trying to intimidate me. "That should tell you that you're not as ready to fight them as you think you are."

"I will not sit here while Astara is out there somewhere." Deep down, I know he may have a good point, but I will not be able to live with myself if the only friend I have gets hurt while I cower and hide.

"You need to feed." The comment startles me from everything else I wanted to say. "Fenrir, leave."

"Right." The Fae spins on his heel like he's planning to do just that.

"Don't you dare, Fae." I feel the nails biting into the skin of my palms.

It's almost comical to see the imposing royal dart his gaze from the vampire to me with a look of panic on his face. I can see the war he fights inside, wanting to do what Zoltan asked and not wanting to piss me off. I watch him from the corner of my eye, not looking away from the damn Daywalker.

"Fenrir." Zoltan's gaze turns smoldering, a knowing smile tilting the corners of his mouth up, showing just a hint of his fangs under it.

The word is punctuated with a blast of power that burns my skin. The punch of it is so sudden it leaves me gasping for air before I'm able to stop myself. With just one look, he has me in a puddle, and I hate it as much as I'm starting to get addicted to the feeling it gives me.

"What in the worlds is going on?" The door opens and Leo pokes his head inside, looking around until his gaze lands on me. His eyes turn into dinner plates.

"This is not happening," Fenrir snaps, bolting for the door and shouldering the shifter out along with him. "They can either fuck or kill each other, I couldn't care less. Karma will be a bitch ..." his voice trails off when the door slams, closing me in a small space with the vampire.

Small space with a bed.

Panic makes me lightheaded and heat pools between my thighs. To make matters worse, Zoltan's nostrils flare. Swallowing thickly, my lips barely move when I call after the Fae. "Coward ..."

"You need to feed." My tongue runs over my teeth at those words. My gums are throbbing.

"I need to shower; I fed already."

"You can feed as you shower." He takes one step closer, the smile growing on his face.

"Umm, no." My breaths are short and too fast, but fuck it. As long as I can talk, I'll try my best to talk my way out of this. "I had enough blood. I need a shower ... only a shower." Damn it, but I don't even believe my own words.

I take a few steps back, not watching where I'm going. Earlier, with all the craziness entering my life with potions and humans alike, I noticed a door there, so I'm guessing it's the bathroom. Whatever it is, I don't care. It is a door. One I can put between me and those blue eyes that want to claim my soul.

A muscle dances on Zoltan's jaw, and his lips press in a thin line when I mention feeding from Fenrir. Well, I fed from a glass, but the vampire doesn't know that. And the fact that it pisses him off makes me all giddy inside, like an idiot with a death wish. What can I say? I'm lucky I'm tough to kill because with logic like mine, I should've been dead many times by now. My head tilts, eyeing the vampire. Maybe he is not wrong for keeping me away from the hunters. Not that I'll admit that to him.

"Go shower." He growls, holding himself stiff as a board. "You'll have to feed from me after unless you want me to rip Fenrir's head off. I can smell his blood in you from here."

"Maybe you should stop sniffing me." I lift a finger up to punctuate my statement and almost run to the bathroom when he growls with an embarrassing squeak. "Asshole!" I lean my forehead on the now-closed door between us when I yell the insult.

He chuckles.

"You really are an asshole." Shaking my head and murmuring under my breath, I blow out a sigh.

He is a tempting destruction as far as destructions go, but I can't let my attraction to him stand in my way. I thought the kidnappings and killings in Sienna were terrible. If I put all the pieces together from everything I've been told, and if it's all correct, someone is trying to bring the hunters across the portal—the same killers that use potions on their blades to make us feral and not remember who we are. The shiver that crawls up my spine is so strong I shake my arms aggressively to ward it off.

"I can hear the wheels turning in your head from all the way out here." Zoltan's voice carries over the door like there is nothing between us. "Shower, then we can talk it over. Whatever it is that's bothering you."

"Will you kill it?" Pushing off the door, I peel my shirt with disgust. "I need clothes, these have to be burned or something." The stench of sweat, blood, and a sweet clawing odor of the potion burn my nostrils when I bring the shirt to my face.

"Will I kill what?" Zoltan focuses on the things that interest him first, typical male. "There are clothes left for you here. I see them at the end of the bed."

"Whatever bothers me, will you get rid of it for me?"

Fighting to keep the smile off my face, I kick off the boots and slide the pants down my hips.

"I get a feeling that's a trick question."

"No one ever accused you of being a dumb bloodsucker." A chuckle escapes me. "Get rid of yourself from the room, will ya? It'll stop bothering me."

"You know that you're not funny, right?" I can hear the smile in his voice contradicting his words.

Fiddling with the taps, I hiss when scolding hot water almost blisters the skin on my hand. The sound of the rushing spray from the showerhead muffles Zoltan's words until I pull my head out of the glass shower.

"I'm fine!" I have no idea why I yell like he can't hear me, and I squeeze my eyes in frustration, rubbing a hand over my face. "I mean, I'm fine," repeating it at a reasonable level, I shake my head at my stupidity. "And I'm very funny. They killed funny in you guys at that damn academy. Trust me on this." Stepping under the warm spray, I sigh, feeling the muscles of my body unclenching one by one, and I continue talking to myself mostly.

"Just being in that place for a short time, I can feel it strangling my funny. It's struggling right now, and I think it'll die a gruesome death if I stay much longer."

Blinking water off my eyes, I grab a bottle and pour shampoo in my cupped hand, breathing in the scent of orange flowers and almonds that overtakes the closed-in space. The glass is all fogged up, giving me a sense like I'm cut off from the world I am in. It's as freeing as it is frightening to look at it that way.

"The academy is not a bad place, Francesca." Zoltan's voice sounds like it's right in my ear, and my heart stops. I can see the dark outline of his body on the other side of the fogged-up glass. "It has been a home, a sanctuary for many of us for many long centuries. Someone is trying to destroy our home. I will not let them."

Lifting my trembling arms, I lather up my hair while keeping a wary eye on the vampire. "It's not my home." The lump in my throat calls me a liar.

"That's where you are wrong," he says softly, and the sadness in his deep voice makes tears prickle my eyes. If he sees it, I'll just blame it on the shampoo. "It's as much your home as you are its home. Soren made sure of that."

"You should be more worried that your sister is missing." He stays quiet for a long moment at my abrupt change of subject.

"She is as old as I am. If anyone can take care of themselves, it's Astara."

We both stay quiet while I rinse off the suds of the shampoo and wash my body. Zoltan doesn't move away, but neither does he enter the shower to join me. He just stands there like a silent sentinel guarding me in my imaginary bubble where I feel falsely safe. I stand under the spray until the water starts running cold, and my fingers and toes prune. At some point, my mind wanders back, going through everything that has led us to this point in time. Shaking off the thoughts, I turn the water off.

"I need a towel." Pulling my hair over my shoulder, I twist it with a vengeance to wring the water out.

"I'm sure this will surprise you, but I've seen a naked female." I laugh at how pride hurt he sounds.

"I'm sure you have seen plenty with that face, but you haven't seen me." Still chuckling, I open the screen door slightly, sticking my hand out, grabbing at the empty air. "And it won't happen today. Towel, please."

He grunts something, but a second later, a piece of thick fabric is pressed into my palm. I pull it inside the shower and open the long, plush towel, wrapping it tightly around me. The tiles are cold on my bare feet when I step out of it, a cloud of steam exiting the shower along with me. I almost run back inside when I see Zoltan looking me up and down with a look of naked hunger on his face. He takes a step towards me.

The door opens with a crash, and Zoltan shoves me behind his back, bracing for an attack.

Fenrir fills up the doorway, a wild look in his gaze.

"It's Astara."

Chapter Fifteen

Zoltan bolts out of the bathroom following Fenrir, and I jump around, shoving my still-wet legs into the pants. The fabric bunches up, sticking to the water, but I pull and twist until I shimmy into them. Yanking the shirt on, stabbing my feet in the boots, I waddle out to follow them and see what's going on. The pants are gaping open, and my unbuckled boots are flapping around as I rush into a sufficiently-spacious living room.

All the furniture is made of dark wood or black stone, contrasting starkly against the white walls. Black and white marble tiles cover the floor, reminding me of a chessboard. It looks modern and sleek, yet everywhere I turn, everything is made of natural material, including the walls. The rough white stone has a sparkle to it that I catch depending on how my head turns. My gaze lands on Fenrir. No one needs to tell me that this place belongs to him. His Fae nature pushes him to natural materials to feel at home, regardless if he is a light or a dark Fae.

Or a freak like me.

I feel more drawn to it as well, which gives me a sense of calm right now that I shouldn't feel. My feet move me closer to where the Fae, Zoltan, and Leo stand around a wide chair. The closer I get, the faster my heart beats. It's her bloodied pants I notice first.

Stopping between Fenrir and Zoltan, my breath catches in my throat at how Astara looks. She's covered in blood from head to toe, her face healing the bruises as I watch. I'm not sure how she managed to get here. The swelling on her eyes is just starting to reside. Remembering my own predicament from earlier that night, I drop on my knees in front of her.

"Call the mage." I sound frantic, but I can't find the strength to hide it. "She must be hurt." Moving my face closer to her, I sniff deeply, looking for that disgusting odor of the potion.

It hits me so hard I gag loudly and turn to the side so I don't puke all over her. My eyes water and saliva fills my mouth while I hack, hoping to remove any trace of it from my nostrils. Fenrir tries to pull me up, but I shove his hands away.

"Call the mage." Snapping at him, I turn to look at all three of them. Gloomy but resolved faces meet my gaze. "I said 'call the mage,' or I'll make it my mission to kill each and every one of you if she turns feral."

"There is nothing a mage can do now." Astara's soft words lack her self-assured attitude, and she sags deeper into the chair with a tired sigh.

"Yes, there is." Stubbornly, I glare at Zoltan in particular. "She's still breathing, which means there is something that can be done. Call the mage for fucks sake. She's your sister. Don't just stand there."

He stares at me so intently that at first, I think he will

argue as usual. It takes a second to see the fear for his sister hiding behind the stony mask. His jaw is set as hard as the marble biting at my knees, and for the first time since I've known him, I can't feel even the smallest trace of his power. Like he is shutting down, lifting the walls around him while expecting the worst, it hits me then that he is also preparing to be the one to end her life. I can literally hear my heart breaking into a million pieces for him. It only solidifies my determination. If those fuckers succeed in this, everything Zoltan is will die right beside his sister.

I will not let that happen.

"Fenrir," I say very calmly, turning my eyes to the Fae, "I need the mage to be here yesterday." He stares at me with a pale face but nods sharply and bolts out of the room, leaving a breeze behind.

"Right." I have two heartbeats, one in my chest hammering away, trying to break my ribs, and another in my throat choking me. "Fenrir said he was bleeding me to get the potion out of my blood." An idea blossoms out of nowhere, and my head snaps in Zoltan's direction. "You tried to reverse my blood flow when Soren cut my hand. It was working, I felt that it was. Can you do it to her, too? Push the potion out instead of letting it spread"

He blinks twice as if waking up from a trance, and I see the life returning, replacing the dull look in his eyes that scares the shit out of me. Leo, on the other hand, stands as still as a statue, his head moving left and right from me to Zoltan. I ignore him for now.

"I can try." It sounds like it hurts him to even say that much. "If she lets me. Her mind is too well trained to allow me to manipulate it."

"She'll let you." Turning to Astara, I grab both her

hands, squeezing so hard I feel the bones of her fingers bending. "Did you hear me? You'll let him."

A strained smile lifts her split lip, but she nods at me with tears in her eyes. I fight my own that prickle and make her face blurry in front of me. Tightening my hold on her, I take a deep breath and allow my fangs to drop. It's either the panic or adrenaline, but whatever it is that causes the magic in my chest to stir, I don't care. I can feel it picking up strength the closer my face gets to Astara's neck. A large hand grabs my shoulder, yanking me back. I hiss at it.

"Are you insane?" Leo snarls in my face, which makes Zoltan growl at him. "You can both go crazy for all I care, but I'm not going to sit here and watch all of you go feral on me. Fuck no." The angrier he gets, the more fur sprouts on his arms and face. "I'll cut her to make her bleed. Don't you dare get those choppers near her. I'll rip your throat out before he can kill me." He stabs a finger at Zoltan.

"I liked you better when you kept your mouth shut." My comment at least makes Astara chuckle weakly, although the wolf just glares at me. "Less talking, more doing." He has a good point, so waving a hand at him, I move aside, letting him take my place. I still keep hold of one of Astara's hands.

Keeping his glower in place, the shifter kneels, pulling a dagger out of his boot. I stiffen when he rips the sleeve from Astara's shirt, exposing her pale, toned arm. When I flick my gaze to her face, I see her watching him with some keen interest that shouldn't be on her face right now. I clear my throat pointedly, and she offers me a sheepish smile as she lifts one shoulder. It would've made me laugh if I wasn't still trying not to freak out.

"Whenever you're ready," Leo growls over his shoulder at Zoltan.

With a nod, the blue color of Zoltan's eyes starts changing, glowing brighter by the second. That same unfamiliar flavor of power I felt the day my life turned upside down saturates the air around us, and a shiver dances over my spine like ghostly fingers. This is not something a vampire—even a pure blood—should have. The knowing comes from somewhere deep inside me, and with it is a feeling that it should tell me something. Something fundamental. It's like trying to grasp water that keeps slipping through your fingers.

Astara hisses when Leo splits the skin of her forearm with the tip of his blade. Red, thick blood mixes with a black, oily substance as it gushes out, soaking Astara's leg. My arm that's pressed to her dig into her skin to speed up the process, and so do the wolf's fingers. Zoltan's power hits me in waves, making it hard to draw a full breath in. I can also hear Astara and Leo taking short breaths as we all stare at the life fluid draining from my friend.

I will tell her that she is my friend after this is over, I decide. I know I should do it now, but I'm selfish and scared. If I voice it out loud and we can't help her, it'll mean I will lose the only real friend I've ever had, and it makes it worse that I never realized this fact before now. Not wanting to go down that road just yet, I turn my thoughts again to the strange feeling inside me. Having my mind occupied makes it easier to handle Zoltan at the moment. The concentration on his face tells me the building can collapse on top of him right now and he won't notice.

Leo makes another cut, Astara's fast healing making it harder on the shifter to keep her bleeding. The grip we have on our hands is firm from both sides, but her fingers are getting slack the longer this goes on. My arm trembles where I squeeze, as if I can physically hold her to this world if I just hold tight enough.

Staring at the red blood dripping on the white tile under the chair brings the face of that hunter to the front of my mind. I welcome it, let my hatred spurn at the sight of him because anything is better than drowning in fear for Astara's life. No matter what they tell me, that hunter is not human —not even a human making a deal with the devil himself. He is something else. Something other. The same knowing from earlier returns, crystalizing his features behind my eyelids. Why do I feel like I should know him? Or know *of* him at any rate.

Going back further in my memories, I try to see if I've ever come across someone like him while working at the agency. Roberti is neck deep in this clusterfuck, so maybe the hunter has been to Sienna? A tremor shakes me at that thought. Have hunters been coming and going through our city? And if that's the case, do they have something to do with the shadows that still give me nightmares?

The door bangs loudly, snapping my eyes open. Fenrir rushes the same male from my room earlier into the room by the scruff of his shirt. When the mage sees me covered in blood again, he backpedals fast, flailing to get away from the Fae.

"Stop it, or I'll kill you now," Fenrir snarls, freezing the poor escape attempt of the male. At my questioning look, his mouth twists unhappily. "I didn't make him forget permanently earlier, just calmed him down a little."

"Kill me," the mage screams, and his hand starts making those weird signs in the air at me again.

I sigh.

"Dude." Using the slang that humans do on their TV, I implore him with my gaze. "My friend needs you. If you do everything you can to help her, you'll never see me again in your life."

I have no idea if what I'm telling him is the truth, but at least the hand movement slows down, and he gapes at me. Remembering my mother and her advice that I should smile more so people don't find me threatening, I make an attempt for Astara's sake.

"You shouldn't exist." The fear is loud and clear in his breathless words.

"Yeah, yeah. I hear that at least once a day. But here I am. And you are still alive with your soul intact." I smile again, letting it slip away when Fenrir shakes his head at me like I'm a naughty child.

I frown at him.

I'm fucking trying here, damn it. I don't see any of them stepping up, and Astara's heart is barely beating anymore. Turning away from the frightened mage, I focus on my friend's face that's as white as the walls around us. Ignoring everyone present, I summon my courage and swallow a lump the size of a fist in my throat.

"I've never had a friend in my life, you know." My words stop the mage's murmuring, and I feel the attention of everyone in the room—including Zoltan, who's not even looking at me. "She pushed her way past the walls I built around myself. For days, she just sat next to me in silence while I ignored her, until I had no other choice but to talk."

Finally looking up, I pin the mage with my tear-filled eyes. "I'm not really friend material, you see. Not many people want a freak like me around them." Winking at him, I pretend I don't feel the fat tear that rolls down my cheek. "But she sat there. Waiting for me to let her in. And I did." My shaking hand moves the bloody strands of hair sticking to Astara's face. "Don't make me lose my friend if you can help … please." My throat closes after that plea.

The silence is so thick in the room that I can cut it with a knife. When I look at everyone one at a time, they stare at me like they've never seen me in their life. Even Zoltan is making me fidget with a look I can't decipher. Heat crawls up my neck, making my face burn. I didn't mean to say all that, but something about the mage and his stupid air signs gets to me. Like I'm some sort of evil here to take his soul or something.

I might be a half blood and a freak. I know I have an attitude that pushes people away, but that's on purpose. No matter what everyone thinks or sees, I know deep in my heart that I'm not evil. Being fast to anger or not putting up with shit doesn't make one full of malice. Him making those weird signs hurt me more than any nasty words thrown my way. Stupid, I know, but it does. And he still hasn't moved to help Astara.

"Let's try it this way." Pulling myself together, I lift my walls back in place. Turning to the mage with an empty stare, I let him see I mean every word of what I'm about to say. "If she dies or turns feral tonight, you will wish for a death that will never come. My face will be the only thing you'll see for eternity."

I guess that is a better motivator. The mage springs into action, rushing in front of Astara but stepping on the other side of the shifter so he is away from me. Like that will save him if she doesn't wake. I watch the blue and green tendrils of his magic swirl between his fingers before they shoot towards Astara, enveloping her in their glow. His hands are twitchy, but that's good. He will try harder if he fears for his life. We all do when the noose is hanging too close to our necks.

Fenrir steps next to me, his energy tentatively poking at mine, and I almost smile. Always the worrier, this one. No matter what I do, he is always there trying his best to make it better. The jerk of Astara's hand pulls my focus on her. Her eyes are still closed, but her mouth opens, fangs growing longer while I watch. We bleed her dry in hopes of taking that damn potion out, and I know what she needs. Not giving anyone time to react, I hug her, yanking the collar of my shirt down and exposing my neck.

Her sharp fangs pierce my throat.

Chapter Sixteen

I'm ripped off Astara, the force almost tearing my throat out. Fenrir is shouting something in the background I can't understand. My mind is a little foggy—okay a lot foggy—but I can't find it in me to regret my decision. She needed blood, and I was willing to give it. Consequences be damned.

A large hand is shoved between my neck and Astara's mouth, prying her jaw open, and whoever it is pulls me away, my limp arms flopping uselessly around my body. I feel like I'm floating, the room spinning around me. Someone cups my head that's hanging listlessly, the back of it touching between my shoulder blades. They lift it up, holding it in place, and Zoltan's face looms in my vision.

"Is she going to be okay?" The words are barely above a whisper, but I know he hears me. He always has a glower on his handsome face whenever I speak.

"I want to kill you myself for doing something so stupid."

And then he kisses the life out of me.

His mouth slams over mine, our teeth clashing when his tongue pushes past my lips. All my senses come to life, and my arms latch around him, my fingers clawing at his shoulders so much you'd think he is trying to get away. His hand tangles in my hair, tilting it to the side so he can ravage my mouth to his liking. I moan deep in my throat, the taste of him sending heat in my belly and wetness between my thighs.

Zoltan pulls me closer, crushing his chest to mine while he sucks my tongue deeper into his mouth. My legs wrap around his narrow hips, pressing his thick erection to my center. My channel clenches empty air, and pings of little shocks force my body to tremble in his arms. Shamelessly, my hips dilute, grinding on him when the sharp tips of his fangs scrape my lips. I need him closer. I need more.

With a tight grip on my head, he jerks me back, pulling his lips away. My eyes snap open, searching his face. He can't be serious if he thinks I'll let him move away. I'll attack him right now if a single one of his muscles even twitches.

Giving me a look that melts my bones, his swollen, glossy lips lift at the corners. I sway in his arms from that alone. His gaze flicks from my eyes to my lips and back a few times, and I can see how painful it is for him to hold back as well. His throbbing erection twitching and straining his pants while bumping against my clit tells me as much, too.

"I need you to feed." His voice sounds more profound than usual, vibrating through his chest into mine. I blink stupidly at him.

That infuriating smirk grows, and he cups my face with his other hand, leaving me hanging on him like a monkey. His rough thumb rubs over my lower lip, pressing it gently.

Poking my tongue out, I swirl it around his finger, not looking away from his face. He groans as if pained.

"You lost too much blood, Francesca." His eyes watch my swirling tongue like it's the most fascinating thing in the world. "I need you to feed ... now."

My heart kicks up when he tilts his head, baring his neck to me. Somewhere at the back of my mind, I'm aware that things must be really bad if he is offering his throat. Even when he stood before me willing to feed me before, he did so with his wrist. Standing in front of me in such a submissive position is nothing like Zoltan.

But I can smell the scent of his skin under my nose.

"Don't make the mistake of thinking I don't want to fuck you right now." His whisper rumbles in my ear. "You are too weak and can't think clearly. When I'm inside you, it'll be with you fully aware. You will remember every moment of it, every inch of me that fills you up. That, Francesca, is a promise. Now feed." He presses my face harder on his skin, and my fangs sink into his flesh.

The precious, powerful blood gushes down my throat— thick and delicious—and I gulp it greedily. My hold on him tightens when I fuse my lips to his skin, and his hips jerk with each hard pull I take. He holds me in place with a hand on the back of my head, but he doesn't need to worry. I have no intention of moving away any time soon. With every second, the fog lifts from my mind. A thought comes to me, smoother and more precise the longer I feed. My hips haven't stopped moving either, and the gyration speeds up as the elastic band in my lower belly tightens.

It snaps so suddenly that my head tilts back hard enough to push away his strong hold on me and a scream so loud it makes my ears ring is ripped from my throat. The bright spots dancing behind my closed eyelids turn dark, the abyss pulling me under. All I can do is sag limply, twitching in his arms. He holds me through it, my head on his shoulder for a long time. It feels like it lasts for days.

I finally open my eyes and jerk back into Zoltan's arms when Fenrir pops his head in my line of sight.

"What the fuck, Fae!"

Reality comes back like a bitch slap to my face when he grins, and Zoltan chuckles.

"I don't find any of this shit funny." Shoving at the damn vampire, I struggle for him to release me.

"She's going to be okay." Fenrir sounds chirpy as fuck, which pisses me off even more. "That was close." He breathes a sigh of relief, and I realize he is not talking to either me or Zoltan.

With dread pooling in my stomach, I twist in the vampire's arms, looking around the room. Every male, the shifter, the mage, and even Fenrir have shit-eating grins on their faces, their pants tenting below the waist. Astara is still sprawled out in the chair, but she is fully awake and thankfully not feral, which the Cheshire-cat smile on her pretty, but still blood smudged face tells me

"That was hot." She snickers under her breath.

I groan.

"You can kill me now." Thumping my head on Zoltan's shoulder, I wish to die when all of them laugh, the vampire's chortle shaking my body in his arms. "This is so embarrassing; I should've just let Roberti kill me." Keeping up with the bumping of my forehead on Zoltan's shoulder, I can't stop talking. "At least Astara is fine. It's worth the show you all got for free. Damn perverted jerks." Which reminds me.

Lifting my face, I turn to the mage that seems too entertained right now. "I see you're not afraid of me anymore." I look pointedly at his crotch.

His face turns beet red, and he folds his hands over his groin. He looks more human than supernatural to me with his unassuming features: crooked nose, thin lips, and eyes set too wide on his face. The longer I stare at him—and the more he fidgets—I can almost see the illusion cast over his appearance.

"I don't know about Roberti, but I would love to get my hands on Cassius," Fenrir growls to my right, reminding me of something that has been nagging me.

"Oh, dear fates, you are right."

Zoltan's thumb is making little circles on the skin of my lower back where the shirt has crawled up, muddling my brain. I clench every time it moves. I can't think, so I jump out of his hold, making us both stumble slightly. He frowns at me, but I ignore him, focusing on the Fae.

"That's what has been bothering me ever since I saw that hunter." All the humor disappears from the room, shrouding us in tension. "He looks like her."

"What?" Fenrir looks worried, like he thinks I've gone insane, so I glare at him.

"The damn hunter I can't get out of my head. Jack, you called him. He looks like her. Cassius's daughter." Fenrir's eyebrows disappear under his hairline. "She was looking at me the same way when she interrupted me with her lackeys. I'll never forget that face."

"She is back at the academy, in Sienna." Zoltan, ever the helpful, points out.

"I never said she wasn't." My voice is as dry as sandpaper, and his scowl deepens. "I said he *looked* like her. Not the lower part of his face ... What's the deal with that anyway?" I look at each of them in turn. "Is his flesh falling off? He looked disfigured under the cover he had on his face."

"You pulled his mask off?" Zoltan stiffens next to me, sucking all the oxygen from the room.

"Yeah …" Eyeing him warily, I inch away slowly. "Why? Is that a big no-no?"

"No one has taken the mask off any of them." Even Fenrir looks troubled.

"Well, that's stupid and on you. You don't have to chase a live one to pull it off. Rip that shit off the face of the dead ones you leave behind instead of burning them to ashes." Reminding him of the fire that blazed in the building, I nod once for emphasis.

"They don't come off, Franky," Astara says softly, a puzzled look on her face. "We've tried many times. It's just part of their face. Like skin."

My head is shaking before she is done talking. "I'm telling you it comes off. I ripped it off and saw his face. Why would I lie to you?"

"No one thinks you're lying," Zoltan growls, staring daggers at all of them as if daring them to contradict him.

I still want to slap him for embarrassing me earlier.

"You are sure he looked like Cassius's daughter?" Leo speaks hesitantly, eyeing Zoltan like the vampire is a snake ready to bite. "She's an only child. His mate died before they could have another. I think that's why she's so spoiled. He let her get away with anything," he grumbles in frustration.

"Unless he is the spitting image of her but not blood related, I say he is something to Cassius. Maybe not a child, but something." I can feel my eyes flicking restlessly, trying to recall both their faces at the same time in my head. "I'm sure of it."

"We need to go back." Fenrir is coiled up for a fight. "You can go home now and better keep your mouth shut. I know where to find you." He snaps at the mage, propelling him into action.

We watch him scatter like a bug, almost tripping over his own feet when he bolts out the door. His mumbled promises are mixed with curses and grumblings about the fates putting a bullseye on his back. It makes no sense to me, so I ignore it, simply watching him leave.

"You should be nicer to him. He saved both of us in one night." I flick a thumb from me to Astara.

"I'm nice enough for allowing him to breathe." Fenrir shocks me with the harshness in his voice. "He shouldn't even be on this side of the portal. I turn a blind eye as long as he does what I tell him to do."

"Well, look at you networking." Putting excitement I don't feel in my words, I watch him grind his teeth.

"Anyway … look." Scrubbing a hand over my face, my lips twist in disgust when I see tainted blood still flaking off it. "I've been thinking, although I must say, until you mentioned Cassius, I couldn't put it together." That gives me everyone's attention. "Seeing that creature's face makes me one-hundred percent sure that he and Cassius are somehow related. There is no doubt in my mind he looks just like his daughter, from the nose up at least. But"—My gaze flicks between all of them in turn—"you said it yourself, the hunters need a mage as old as dirt to have a potion as deadly as the one they are using. Isn't Cassius a mage?"

Fenrir opens his mouth, and I know what he wants to say before I hear it.

"He already turned his back on all of you and attacked you two. He is capable of doing it, isn't he?" When the Fae closes his mouth with an audible snap, I know I'm right.

"We have shadows devouring innocents on the streets in Sienna. Guards are dropping dead on the grounds of the academy." I lock gazes with Leo, remembering his beta. His animal stares at me through his eyes. "Who else knows our home"—Turning to Zoltan, I throw his words back at him —"better than him? An outsider can't hide evidence as well as they've done without being intimately away from everything and everyone. It's him, I know it. He has infiltrated the academy to bring us all down."

"To what end?" Astara sounds like she'll be sick.

"I don't know." I flick my eyes to Zoltan, again. "He was your friend; you tell me."

"We need to go." Fenrir starts moving towards the door. "Now!"

Chapter Seventeen

Walking out from the building where Fenrir's apartment is on the top floor, I look around, stretching my eyes as open as they'll go so I can see everything. It's bad timing to be excited about seeing the human world, I know, but finally, it hits me that I'm not home. I'm in this strange place—one I only ever thought fictional since I could see it through the TV screen.

But I'm here.

Even this late in the night, when darkness is streamed with lighter shades of gray and dawn is near, humans walk around the busy streets. Sadness passes over me like a gentle wave when I glance up and all I see is a bright gray sky. The moon is not where it always is. The silver orb in the sky that greets me every time back in Sienna, the same one I constantly take for granted shining her love on my skin.

"You okay, Franky?" Astara saddles close to me, linking her arm through mine. "You look … sad." Her reluctant tone pulls my gaze her way.

"Do you see the moon here often?" A line forms

between her perfect eyebrows, her face now clean from blood and gore, at least. "I can't see anything from the bright lights and tall buildings in this human world. It's weird to see a sky erased from everything that makes it special." My hand waves up, pointing at the blank gray canvas above our heads. "Not even stars."

"Ah, that." Nodding in understanding, she pulls me to walk faster through the streets with storefronts that have big glass displays, bright white lights illuminating the sidewalk we are using. "Humans are not fond of dark places. I sometimes think it must be the times before the Purge that make them so obsessed with light." Grinning at me, she wiggles her eyebrows. "The dark and the night is where we are at home. Where we lurk."

"They must think all of us are evil and want to slaughter each and every one of us." Keeping my eyes on Zoltan's back I watch his purposeful stride as the Fae and the shifter flank each of his sides. My thoughts stray, pulling out random things, but I try not to focus on them. "With everything that we've been dealing with lately, I can't blame them."

"They worry about their pathetic short lives as if they'll achieve I don't know what in the blink of an eye." She dismisses my comment nonchalantly, and my gaze snaps to hers.

"You can't really mean that." At my harsh words, she pulls back, watching me as if I've slapped her. "From where I'm standing, they've achieved quite a lot for such a pathetic, short life. And wouldn't you want to live to the fullest if your time was short? I know I would."

"They fear what they don't understand is what I was saying." Astara gets defensive, but I don't stop her. I don't like how she dismisses human lives the same way supernaturals dismiss the lives of half-bloods like me. "In their history, do you know how many innocents have been killed just for being different? Including supernaturals like us. Their witch trials were a clear example. They slaughtered mages and innocent human women alike."

"You mean the same way someone is slaughtering our kind now in Sienna?" She opens her mouth to speak, but I talk over her. "The same way half-bloods have always been killed for being different? I still can't see the difference between them and us."

A loud honk from a passing car makes my heart jump in my throat, and Zoltan looks over his shoulder, locking his gaze on mine immediately. Shaking my head slightly, I offer him a small smile. He searches my gaze for a moment before turning back with a slight nod. I know all three of them can hear every word I say, but I don't care. There's nothing in this life I hate more than hypocrites.

We go quiet, Astara and I, still with our linked arms following the males through this city. It's … nice. Strangely, I start noticing the humans we pass giving us wary glances, and that causes my skin to prickle. Fenrir casts his illusion to hide us from view, what happened when the hunters attacked us, and no one saw anything, confirmed it that his illusions work in this world. So why are the humans either inching away or looking like they want to start tearing our clothes off? The hunger in their eyes is undeniable.

My mouth opens so I can point it out to everyone when fingers wrap around my swaying forearm, stopping me in my tracks. The hold is over the sleeve on my shirt, but it still irks me enough that I whirl at whoever dares touch me. I come face to face with a human male staring at me like he is a second away from pulling me in the dark alley between the buildings at our back.

My head cocks to the side and I watch the human, fascinated that he looks as muscled and as tall as the males with us. Dark tattoos peek from under the collar of his shirt and cover his arms to his wrists. I let him hold my forearm as I scan him from head to toe, noticing the fabric of his jeans stretching over muscular thighs and his white shirt straining over his broad, barreled chest. His skin is tan, like melted chocolate, while his dark brown eyes stare at my face with unbridled lust. The features on his face are not as perfect as the supernaturals, but the little imperfections on it, like his thinner upper lip or his little, too-square jaw, make him more appealing somehow.

"What the hell ..." Astara startles, gaping at the human and me.

"You are the most beautiful thing I have ever seen." The human speaks, taking a step closer while pulling me to him at the same time.

"You know I'm not human?" My head tilts to the opposite side. I'm finding this particular human very fascinating.

"What?" eyebrows rising up, he pulls back with a jerky shake of his head, some of the lust disappearing from his chocolate eyes.

"You called me a thing." My chin lowers, and I stare at him, judging if he is all there. I did hear him say 'thing' to me. Did he forget what he was saying?

Astara moves, probably to do her mind screwing on him and make him go away, but I yank her back with the hold on our linked arms. This is very strange, the human talking to me. I don't want her to interfere.

"You should come with me," the human tells me, jerking hard on my forearm and wrapping his other arm around my waist.

Coming face to face with him, I see that I am right. He

is as tall as me, and taller than most humans I've seen. He also smells different. Not as overwhelming as the suit guy I wanted to attack when they first brought me to this world, but just as enticing. I can feel Zoltan's power blast me at my back, and I know he has noticed something is off, which means my time is up.

"If you don't let go of me, you are in big trouble." Grinning at the startled look on his face, I see the golden flakes in his irises while we stand with our noses almost touching.

The human is ripped away from me, his feet leaving the ground when Zoltan grabs him by the neck. My skin burns from the rage blasting off the vampire, who is dangling the poor male like a dog with a chew toy. The human's face turns a bright shade of purple and veins bulge in his thick neck, and Zoltan keeps squeezing, luckily not hard enough to separate his head from his body.

"Don't kill him." Placing my hand on Zoltan's arm, I shake him. "You can't kill this one."

"Yes, I can. Watch." The jerk growls, his fingers tightening around the human's neck.

"No, Zoltan. Please." I think it's the please that does the trick because he finally stops. He turns his head to glare at me, and I know the human can't breathe right now, so I need to convince him fast. "There is something about him. You can't kill him. He is not like the rest of the humans." When that doesn't help, I hurry to add. "He smells different. See for yourself."

Zoltan doesn't look happy, although he turns around, bringing the human closer from where he dangles him at arm's length. I hold my breath and wait to hear if I'm right. I have no idea why I find this so important. The air around us shimmers, and I hear Fenrir cursing up a storm somewhere behind me.

"Oh, shit." Astara groans, and the human rasps at the same time.

At least that means the human can breathe.

I turn my head, wanting to see what got the Fae to use such inventive language, and my stomach drops to my feet. Fenrir's eyes are glowing, his long blond hair dancing in an imaginary breeze around his head. Leo's body is contorting, twisting at awkward angles as he shifts to his wolf form. Astara is crouched, facing something I can't yet see. At least the humans that were staring at us seem to be ignoring our presence again. All but the one rubbing a hand over his neck, watching us with wide eyes.

"What's going on?" My instincts take over, and I stand in front of Zoltan and the human, ready for an attack.

"Hunters," Astara growls.

"I thought they couldn't see us." Frustrated, I scan the street where humans walk around without a care in the world.

"They broke through my illusion." Fenrir spins in a slow circle, and the air around us shimmers again.

"That's why the humans could see us." I feel responsible if anyone gets hurt now. I should've said something when I noticed them staring. "Well, he can still see us." Fenrir glares at the human I'm pointing at as if it's his fault the hunters broke through his illusion. "Stay away from that human, Fae."

Ignoring the daggers Zoltan is staring at my back, I roll my shoulders. Whatever the reason the human can see us, he is different, and I feel strangely protective of him. A tremor races up my spine when I see white-clad people from the corner of my eyes slinking through the streets. My face lifts, and I notice them on the roofs of the slightly lower buildings.

"We are being surrounded." Glancing behind me at Zoltan, I point at the top of a building.

"No one fights." Zoltan turns away from the human stepping next to me. "We get to the portal. There was enough fighting for one night." We all watch him like he's lost his mind. "We can fight another day; we need to get back now. Jack knows you saw his face. I have a feeling the academy needs us more than we need to kill a few hunters."

"Okay."

Astara is first to agree, and I can't help but wonder if getting hurt messed with her head. I've gotten myself in so many situations where my life was on the line that it would be shocking if this one in the human world screwed with my head. My friend is strong—the top of the food chain, if you will—and I have a feeling she doesn't get hurt often.

"Run." Zoltan snaps and, grabbing my hand, he bolts down the street.

I look over my shoulder at the human we are leaving behind, clutching his thighs and gasping for air. His eyes find mine, and I almost trip over my own feet from the speed of Zoltan's run. We turn a corner, and I lose sight of him. Fear for his life makes me slower than I should be, and I know Zoltan is getting frustrated. Shaking off the worry, I push harder and it makes me faster as I release the vampire's hand and follow the others.

The city blurs around us. My unbraided hair streams behind me like a flag, the long strands flapping and yanking on my skull. Not knowing where I need to go, I make sure I don't lose sight of Astara or Fenrir. Leo is long gone, the shifter bolting as soon as Zoltan says we won't fight. Breathing through my mouth to avoid gagging from the stench of all the odors in the city, a smile stretches my lips. It's exuberating to run for your life. Being reminded that death is at your heels even when you live for centuries is good for the soul. You appreciate life more. At least I do.

The surroundings become familiar, and I can feel the pull of the portal near. My heart speeds up knowing that safety, as feeble as it is, is just a few moments away. Fenrir stops dead in his tracks, and I have to twirl to not topple over him, stopping only a breath away from Astara. Zoltan is next to me before I stop moving. Anger bubbles in my chest.

Two rows of white-clad hunters block our way to the passage home. There are about forty of them that I can count with a glance, and my heart pummels my ribs with abandon. Now that I'm closer to the academy, even with a portal separating me from it, I feel the ancient magic stirring in my chest. I'm giddy to get home. *You and me both*, I tell the monstrosity that lives inside me. *Just not yet.*

"I guess we get one more fight out of it before we leave." My attempt to lighten the situation falls on deaf ears. "Umm, where is Leo?"

The area where the portal sits unknown to humans is halfway up a hill. There is a tall metal tower just to the side of it with a couple of wooden benches placed in weird spots. A small forest surrounds the clearing, and two hiking paths branch off, going up and down the hill. If the trees were taller and thicker, it would look like a replica of the one that sits on the other side of the academy. Not very inventive, are we?

Astara points at something interrupting my observation, and I follow the direction of her finger.

"He is insane." My body stiffens when I catch a glimpse of fur waving through the trees close to the portal. "Is he trying to get killed, or worse?"

"He can get through if we give him an opening."

Zoltan's words are just a whisper, and I realize I never asked if the hunters have our hearing. "He can bring help from the other side. We just need to keep them occupied until then."

"Jack is not here." Zoltan looks at me sharply from the disappointment in my voice, and I barely stop myself from flinching. "That fucker is mine." Putting as much bravado as I can summon into my voice, I ignore his low growl. "I guess these idiots will do for now."

"Don't underestimate the hunters, Ms. Drake." If possible, I think steam will shoot from my ears in this moment. He did not just call me Ms. Drake again.

"I never underestimate anyone, oh mighty Daystalker—I mean Daywalker." Giving him the sweetest smile ever, I see him flinch. Good! "It's usually everyone else underestimating little ol' me." My mind is already spinning with possibilities, and I can only think of one idea that might actually work as I'm eyeing the trees around us.

"Can they see as good as we can?" I turn to Fenrir, ignoring the bloodsucking jerk.

"Better than humans, but not as good as us. Why?" I don't hear the rest of what he says, and I do my best to ignore his hiss as I swagger out of the cover of the trees and out into the open.

All eyes turn on me, including the three sets staring at my back.

"Hey, ugly fucks!" Spreading my arms wide like I want to give them all a hug, I grin crazily at the hunters. "Who's up for a chase? Come get me if you can."

Chapter Eighteen

More than half of the hunters peel off from the rest, giving chase. I'm sure if I give them time to think they will see how stupid of a plan it is, but I'm sure they expect us to be stealthy and try to surprise them with our attack. It's something Zoltan and Fenrir would do. Assess your opponent, find weak spots, and pick them off.

My time in this world—as short as it is—and the attack I barely survived has taught me one thing: the hunters have learned the patterns, the way we fight, and how we think. Good thing they have me now with my act-and-then-think attitude.

And they say I'm crazy.

My wild laughter bounces off the tree trunks and echoes around the hill as I bolt for the tree line to my right. Leo is slinking on the left, so this should give him the opening *Mr. jerk* wants for him. Throwing a glance over my shoulder, a large chunk of my hair nearly blinding my left eye when it slaps me over it, I manage to see a tail near the swirling portal before ducking to avoid a dagger aimed at my head.

"That's what you get, Franky, for being cocky." Snorting at myself, I ignore the piece of hair that got sliced up, floating to the forest floor.

"I'd say the same thing." Zoltan snarls from next to me.

I bare my teeth at him in the mockery of a smile. "You're welcome."

"This is not what I meant." Grabbing my arm, he tugs me to the side, plastering both of our backs behind a good-sized tree trunk. "You need to stop acting out of control and listen for once."

"Ms. Drake." Blowing the hair out of my face, I inch closer to the edge, poking my head out to see if the hunters are near.

"What?"

"Stop growling." Huffing, I snatch the elastic band from my wrist, tying up my hair. "You forgot to add Ms. Drake at the end." Not so accidentally, I elbow him in the process just because.

"Is that what all this is about?"

"You don't get to kiss the life out of someone, hump them like a horny dog twice, and call them Ms. Drake, Zoltan." I thrust my head out again when a branch cracks nearby. "That's not how shit works. I don't do hot and cold well."

"Meeting you was bad timing, that's all." His sigh makes me look at his face. "People are dying, and I'd rather you not be one of them if I can help it. We have time for everything after this is over."

"Don't mistake this for what it's not. After this is over, I'll be gone, and you, pure blood, need to find your mate." A lump forms in my throat, but I push it down forcefully. "I have other shit to do ... half blood stuff, you know."

"Francesca ..."

The air changes density so suddenly I throw both of us to the side, avoiding the shuriken that sticks almost all the way in the tree. There is a strange lurch inside me, making my breath stick in my chest. I feel like I'm going to puke. Everything around me spins for a split second when Zoltan yanks me to my feet, and then the early night and the forest come to life in brilliant, bright colors. A calm settles on my shoulders, and it's very different than the one that pulls me into the trance-like state when my heartbeat slows down.

Zoltan sucks in a sharp breath through his teeth.

"My eyes changed, didn't they?" He nods once, watching me with worry he shouldn't feel right now. I tell him as much. "Just make sure you don't get hurt. I'll be back."

I'm grateful he doesn't try to stop me. The colors swirl, dancing happily around me like they are excited I can finally see them. Everything has a different note to it, even the dirt under my feet pulses with a light of its own. Dark blotches through the bright green of the trees point at the hunters gliding through the forest towards the place where Zoltan is. I can see five of them close by, with a handful getting closer but still further back.

Grabbing a low branch, I pull myself up the tree. My feet barely make a sound as I run over the thicker ones, jumping from one tree to the other, and as if I weigh nothing, not a leaf rustles from my movements. Stopping above the first dark shape, my fangs drop from my gums. Reaching down, I yank the hunter up, ripping his throat out as soon as we are face to face.

I leave him hanging like a wet towel on the branch, his blood dripping and soaking up the dry dirt at the gnarled roots. That thing in my chest vibrates, not with excitement, but with something that I can't name. Excitement is definitely not what I feel right now. More like collecting old debts ... a sacrifice long overdue. I keep moving like a ghost through the forest, leaving hunters decorating the trees like ornaments swaying on the branches. The light of the forest floor gets more vibrant, the lifeblood feeding the hunger it feels. *It must've been parched,* I think dispassionately.

One by one, the dark blotches disappear, leaving the life of everything around me swirling in harmony once again. I see I've circled back to where I started, and I crouch on my perch in the tree, watching Zoltan from above. His chest is rising and falling with even breaths, and every muscle on his body is corded, coiled up for an attack. The stark beauty of his face in this new world of swirling lights makes him look angelic.

A devil in disguise, if you will.

He will make a perfect mate for some lucky female—a fact I try to ignore because he awakens everything female inside of me. It is nice when I let myself believe he can be mine, but for some reason reality—the bitch she is—slaps me in the face tonight. Go figure. The thought squeezes my chest in a vice, and my heart does a painful thump against my ribs. The colors disappear, leaving me in total darkness. Blinking rapidly, I finally see the light gray shapes from my normal vision.

The branch cracks slightly under my weight.

Zoltan's head snaps up, his gaze locking on mine, and I smile at the frown on his face. Wrapping both hands on the rough bark of the tree, I swing myself down, dangling for a second before dropping on the ground.

"All clear." Dusting off my hands on my pants, I blow a breath through pursed lips. "You think Leo had time to go through?" He keeps staring at me, so it's my turn to frown. "What?"

Without saying a word, he steps in front of me, cupping my face. My heart stops beating as I watch him, my eyes widening. The harsh, cutting lines on his face soften, and pulling his shirt out of his waistband, he lifts it to my face. My eyes focus on the ridges of his abs and firm pecks. His torso looks like the skin is stretched over granite, emphasizing every muscle under it. Who knew there were so many of them in the upper body? I follow the bumps and dips hungrily while he gently wipes the blood off my face. I must be a mess, so it is no wonder he gives me that strange expression.

"We should go find Astara and Fenrir." I have the strangest urge to place the palm of my hand on his chest and feel his deep voice vibrating under my skin.

I clench my fists.

"Lead the way." Taking a step back, I'm relieved and upset with myself. I should not feel like this. I'm going to force myself to stop, I decide.

He searches my face, dropping his shirt and leaving it sticking above his waist, showing just a bit too much skin for my sanity. Gingerly, with only two fingers, as if I'm touching a poisonous snake, I pull it over his abs, petting it a couple of times for good measure. Not that I want to touch him. No. Not at all. I just need to make sure it stays down.

Right, I almost convince myself, too.

Spinning on my heel, I head in a random direction. The stronger the pull from the portal gets, the more I know I'm going to the right place. I can feel Zoltan 's eyes on my back the whole time, making me stumble a few times. Instead of watching where I'm going, I'm too busy paying attention to him. The tops of my boots bump and snag on quite a few rocks and dips on the ground.

"Very graceful, Franky. You're so stupid," murmuring under my breath, I start stomping forward.

"What's stupid?" the distraction from behind me asks.

"Nothing, never mind." I flinch internally when I snap at him. It's not his fault I have no control over my ovaries.

"Francesca …" I hate it, absolutely hate it when he says my name with the hint of that damn accent.

"Are we going to confront Cassius's daughter as soon as we get back?" Silence follows my question, and I ignore the stabbing I feel from his gaze between my shoulder blades.

"We need to be careful about how we approach this," he says after an eternity of only hearing the sound of our feet on the forest floor.

"I say we watch her every move for a day or two. See what she's up to, you know." A sigh passes my lips when he goes along with the change of subject. "You'll be surprised what people do when they think no one is watching."

"Yes, you would be surprised." There is something in the way he says the words that makes me look at him over my shoulder.

"It's creepy to stalk people, you know that right?" The smirk is back on his face, and it sends a zing through my stomach. "You are a fucking creep."

"Says the one that wants to stalk students at the academy."

"Hunters don't look like me, asshole. So, don't spin it to suit you." Scowling at him, I barely sidestep a hole in the forest floor that would've sent me face first on the ground.

It pisses me off more.

"No, you just came to the academy under false pretenses in hopes to spy for an organization we later discovered works against all of us."

Well, when he puts it like that …

"I had nothing to do with it and was manipulated as much as everyone else. You know that, so don't give me that bullshit."

"I didn't accuse you of anything. I'm just stating the facts that made watching you a priority." The amusement in his voice grates on my nerves. "Or stalked, as you like to call it."

"Whatever." My feet speed up. I want to get as far away from him as possible right now.

I see Astara first. Her head pokes out from behind a tree, her gaze locking on ours. The harsh look on her face is replaced with a smile when she comes out, followed by a very put-out Fenrir. I almost laugh at the expression on his face. Until he rushes, yanking my feet off the ground. I dangle in his hands, staring down at him.

"You are a reckless, insufferable female, Francesca Drake," Fenrir hisses, giving me a hard shake for emphasis.

"That's old news, you'll have to come up with something new if you want me to act surprised." Grinning at him, I shake my head. "Now put me down or I'll kick you in your teeth. No one likes a pretty boy with no front teeth, trust me."

Astara chortles, and Zoltan even chuckles, seeming surprised that I made him laugh. Only the Fae doesn't crack a smile, but I know he is laughing inside. No way am I not funny. He is just a killjoy like Argoz. My feet are finally lowered on the forest floor.

"Did Leo go through?" Turning from Astara to Fenrir, I roll my shoulders, which are cramped from when the damn Fae tried to act like a gorilla. Males!

"Did he ever," Astara says excitedly, grabbing my arm and pulling me with her to the end of the tree line.

"You did awesome, Franky!" She claps her hands in glee.

Dead hunters litter the ground around the portal. Wolves the size of a horse stand over them like hounds from hell protecting their prey. I see Leo's wolf poised at the center of the swirling lights, his upper lip lifted over deadly jaws in a snarl. Those intelligent green eyes find me, scanning me up and down through his animal face. The shifters didn't do anything I didn't, yet seeing all the death in front of me makes me sick.

Hopefully things are better on the other side, but something about the way the shifter is standing tells me I won't like what I find.

Chapter Nineteen

This time it feels less horrible when I cross the portal. It might be because I am already feeling sick to my stomach on the other side but I'm not sure. It all fades when I tilt my head up, the silver moonlight washing over my face like a caress. *Home,* the voice inside my head whispers with reverence.

"We have a problem." Argoz shouts, coming around the monstrosity of the building as he rushes to meet us. I know it's terrible because the ghoul is yanking on the collar of his shirt, leaving it gaping at the neck. Exchanging a tired look with Astara, we head his way, Zoltan, Fenrir, and Leo—who's still in wolf form—trailing behind us. Everyone knows I've always been a workaholic, not wanting to deal with actually thinking about anything, burying it all to keep busy, but this is getting to be too much. Even for me.

I need a break from life …

"We are okay, thank you for asking." I greet him dryly, not stopping when he startles at my comment.

"That is a piece of excellent news, indeed, Ms. Drake."

Wringing his hands, he seems torn about whether to follow us or wait for the males. "Unfortunately, we have a situation here to deal with, so we can't pause to celebrate your first passage between the worlds."

"You actually do that?" Ignoring Argoz, we continue on our way. "Celebrate when someone goes through for the first time?"

"You saw what happened." Astara shrugs. "It's kind of like a rite of passage." Argoz grunts something, turning away from us.

"Hmmm, interesting." I don't find anything interesting about it, but at least I prolong the time of my ignorance. I really don't want to hear what problems the ghoul is talking about.

Snorting, Astara bumps her shoulder with mine. "You know he will follow us around until he speaks his mind, right? It's one thing I love and loathe about Argoz. Insistent like a pest."

"It's not like we are going to run away. I tried, remember? That shit doesn't work." A muscle twitches between my shoulders at the thought. "We will face it as soon as we enter the building. He didn't have to come all the way here." Cracking my neck, I rub it with my hand. "I'm so tired that I could probably sleep for a century or two."

"I hear ya on that." She sounds as tired as I feel.

"It'll have to wait." Fenrir joins us with a sigh. "Three more disappearances in Sienna, two dead guards found in the hallways near their rooms …"

"You just couldn't wait, could you?"

"And two of the vampire students were found decapitated in the dining hall." The Fae gives me a side-eye glance.

"How many of them are there?" Pushing away the

fatigue dragging me down, my brain kicks back into gear. "Hunters," I clarify when both of them look at me with a question on their faces. "Between the first attack and those we had waiting for us in front of the portal, I thought that was the majority of them?" Phrasing it as a question, my head turns from Astara to Fenrir. "It was close to seventy? Maybe?"

"That's about half of their organization in the city, yes." When my eyebrows crawl up my forehead, Fenrir shakes his head. "They are scattered around the world, close to the portals we have. This is not the largest one they have." He turns to Astara, asking for confirmation with his gaze. "I think that's London, no?"

"Yes, their numbers are greater there." Nodding absent-mindedly, she stares with distant eyes at the academy. "Although, if Zoltan goes through this portal a couple more times in a row, we might find them coming in waves."

"Oh, goody." At least I'm not the only one obsessed with the jerk. It doesn't make me feel better, either.

"I'm more worried if Francesca is seen going through right now." Fenrir's comment makes me frown at him.

"Why? What did I do? The assholes were attacking us. Should I have just sat there meekly?" My fists clench. "What I did at the portal might have been a little over-board, I'll give you that much, but at least no one ended up poked with a potion-soaked dagger."

A look passes between them.

"What?" Astara chuckles when I snap at them.

"We are worried …"

"We?" I stare at her pointedly, and she nods.

"Yes, we are worried about you being seen going through because they now know that you are his weakness," she says it gently, as if it will hurt less that way.

"Excuse you?" I can't believe what I'm hearing, so I stop walking, glaring at both of them. "How the fuck did the two of you come to the conclusion that I'm his weakness? Because I saved his ass from being skewered a few times?"

"Exactly." Fenrir nods primly at me, and I want to slap the arrogant expression off his face.

"You should get your head checked, Fae." Shouldering my way past him, I march towards the open double doors of the academy, murmuring under my breath. "I'm his fucking weakness, my ass. He has no weakness apart from being a jerk, that's what that is."

"My brother does not get skewered." Astara must've followed my rushed footsteps.

"Well, he almost did."

"That's my point exactly, Franky." My stomping slows down at that. "He is looking after you more than watching his own back. It leaves him open most of the time."

My stupid heart jumps at that.

"Soren tied my life to this academy, and your lives, so he is protecting his interest, you could say." Take that stupid heart.

"If you say so." She doesn't sound happy at my reasoning, but I don't care. That should strangle my ovaries and put them in their place. "But my point is, he doesn't pay attention with you around. They are going to explore that after seeing it."

"There is a solution for that." My hand waves animatedly so she can't see it trembling. "Keep him away from me. He is a pain in my ass, anyway. Problem solved."

Stepping through the doors, we both stop when heads turn our way. Some of the faces seem relieved to see us, but a few are watching us with hatred burning in their eyes. For the hundredth time, I can't help but wonder what I've ever done to any of them, apart from being alive. It's not news that everyone hates half-bloods, but they can at least ignore me.

"I think the two of you should come along." Fenrir walks by, not even turning to see if we will follow.

I want to go in the opposite direction on principle alone, just so he knows he can't boss everyone around. The tense atmosphere, along with the energy in this place that pumps like a ticking bomb, move my feet to follow his lead. Everyone is tracking our movements in dead silence, making me uneasy. I don't like being the center of attention unless it's a fight. I want to get fucking superstar attention in a fight.

We pass the hallways, flames dancing above our heads like they are happy to see us. I look at my feet so I don't have to see everyone staring, and a frown pulls on my forehead. No wonder they are staring. Glancing at Astara, I see she is wearing the same clothing from when she was hurt. We both are painting a picture like we have bathed in blood. The garments are black, but there is no mistake why it's all stiff and crusted, the stench wafting off us confirming it loud and clear. My head lifts and I grin at a demon guard we are passing, the wildness in my eyes making him flinch.

"Stop that." Astara snickers, and I join her despite my effort to not smile.

"They'll stare anyway." Shrugging a shoulder, I scan the place around, but my mind is in a different place. "This will give them something to talk about."

Fenrir heads to a room on our right, stepping inside and holding the door open for the rest of us. We all pile in, spreading around. It's a comfy-looking space with bookshelves lining the walls, a desk pushed in one corner with a leather chair behind it. A few sofas are scattered around, and some armchairs, giving everyone space enough to take seats.

I rush to an empty chair so no one can sit next to me, making Astara laugh at me. Groaning, I curl my legs under me, every muscle in my body hurting. Even the ones I didn't know existed. My tailbone hurts for fuck's sake. I can't remember if I fell on my ass anywhere. Zoltan sits behind the desk—I mean, of course he does. At my scrunched-up face, Astara chortles again, covering it with a cough.

"So, things have escalated while we were gone." Zoltan addresses Argoz, who is the only one standing. Well, he didn't fight for his life that I know of.

"Yes, as I told you, and we found no evidence pointing us in any direction." The ghoul yanks his shirt collar. "The Board was notified, but we haven't heard anything from them yet. Soren is still unresponsive."

That perks up my ears.

"Everyone was accounted for at the time?" Argoz frowns at my question.

"Yes, the guards questioned and checked on everyone."

"And who questioned and checked on the guards?"

"We did, of course." He glares at me, acting insulted.

"You can glare all you want, ghoul. Someone inside here is picking us off one by one. Excuse me for questioning how thorough you lot are." Grinding my teeth, I stab the air with a finger, pointing at the closed door. "Those fuckers out there mean business. This was the first time I've come across them that I know of, and I nearly died." His eyes widen comically. "Astara nearly died thanks to them. They are upping their game to whatever their end goal is. Meanwhile, here we are, holding conferences."

"I assure you, Miss Drake, I wish to find them as much as you do." Spreading his arms wide, he appears defeated, and guilt stabs me for going off at him. "There is only so much I can do."

"Francesca, we know Argoz has our best interest at heart. You are placing your anger in the wrong place," Fenrir says softly, while Zoltan watches me with an unreadable look on his face.

I squirm in my seat.

"I'm angry at many things, but Argoz is not one of them." There is tension in my neck, and no matter how many times I crack it, I can't get it to go away. "I'm just … I'm … tired." I sink deeper into the chair with a sigh.

"We all are, and we need rest." Zoltan leans his forearms on the desk. "There is not much any of us can do right now, and I suggest we all get some sleep. It was a long night." Turning to Argoz, he nods in acknowledgment. "For all of us."

"What do they all have in common?" blurting it out, I glance at all of them in turn. "They must be somehow connected, right?"

"They are all random." Argoz doesn't sound very sure.

"We figured out that all the killings and disappearances in Sienna were half-bloods." When Azgor opens his mouth, I stop him with a hand. "It's okay, you can say it in front of me. It's what I am and I can't change that." I turn to Zoltan and Fenrir. "The rest must be somehow connected. They were pure bloods for sure?"

"The guards and students, yes." Fenrir nods thoughtfully, searching my face. "What are you thinking?"

"From everything I know so far, it all leads me back to this academy." I watch them all, chewing on the inside of my mouth. "They were looking for a freak throughout Sienna, hoping for dragon blood, or so we think. After I got manipulated inside the gates, guards started dropping like flies. Now, students have joined the headcount, and only vamps. The only ones that are actually Daywalkers."

"That's fishing," Zoltan points out with a stony face.

"If you ask me, it's too much of a coincidence." Rubbing my thighs roughly, I lift off the chair. "I don't like coincidences, nor do I believe in them." Ignoring the pointed stare Zoltan gives me, I turn around, heading for the door.

"Get some rest," Fenrir calls out when I jerk the door open.

"I'll rest when I'm dead." Looking over my shoulder, I give him a strained smile." I have shit to do."

"Where are you going?" Astara leans forward as if preparing to follow me.

"I have to see an annoying old man about something. If you hear him scream, I might've stabbed him to wake him up."

Astara's laughter follows me even after I close the door behind me. Soren better be in a chatty mood. I'm not joking when I say I'll stab his ass if he doesn't wake up.

Chapter Twenty

"Francesca." Zoltan's voice stops me at the entrance of the golden hallway—a nickname I came up with all on my own. I stop at the weapons room first; I like to be prepared for the conversation I'm about to have.

"There are things that only Soren knows, Zoltan. I have to try." Watching his long legs eating up space between us makes me inch closer to the hallway, knowing he can't enter. "I can't just sit and hope for the best."

"I'm not trying to stop you." One side of his mouth quirks up at my suspicious squint. "I'm not."

"What do you want, then?"

"I heard what Astara and Fenrir were saying."

"Instead of eavesdropping, you should've paid more attention to what Argoz was saying." Annoyed, I fidget from one foot to the other. "You know, about people being killed and all that. Then what I said would make more sense to you, and you wouldn't call it fishing."

"You are angry with me."

"Do you even hear yourself when you talk?" My heart

picks up a beat to match my frustration. "Not everything is about you. People are dying, for fuck's sake. No one is doing anything about it except talk, and then they talk some more. Well, I'll be damned if I sit on my ass and let it happen."

"They are wrong." He keeps with his one-track mind, ignoring everything I said. "You are not my weakness."

"So, you didn't almost get stabbed and pinned to a wall like an entomology project gone wrong?"

"I'm not an insect." He growls through clenched teeth.

"No, you're just a jackass." I rub a hand over my face tiredly. "Listen, can we do this another time? Like maybe next year, huh?" At his glower, I sigh. "I want to see if Soren will talk to me, and then I want to sleep. I can't even think straight anymore."

"We need to talk about this." Repeating the same thing like a broken record, his hand reaches for my face, freezing in midair when I flinch. "Make no mistake that we will talk about whatever this is, Francesca Drake."

My heart is jackhammering in my chest as I watch him storm away. My eyes burn with unshed tears that I angrily blink away. We won't be doing jack shit if I stay away from him. I managed to do it after the party that screwed up my life, and I'll do it again. The longer I think about it, the more determined I get.

Spinning on my heel, I face the hallway. It stretches in front of me as far as my eyes can see. I feel its call like a gentle touch at the center of my chest, unlike at the beginning when it was overwhelming. It's more like a greeting than a call. With a deep breath, I step through the invisible border that no one can cross if Soren doesn't want them too. I need to ask him for pointers on that one; it'll come in handy.

My feet move slowly, and I watch my fingers trail over

the golden accents of the decorative molding on the wall. The tips of my nails bump the divots and swirls, twisting up like the waves of an ocean. It's soothing being here in this place of mystery, and I feel my body relaxing with each breath I take. It's not long before I find myself standing in front of Soren's door. I just stop, staring at it like the wood will tell me all the secrets I want to know.

The door cracks open.

"It's good to know I'm welcomed." Pushing with the palm of my hand, I walk inside. "I was beginning to think you didn't want to see me."

Silence is my answer, the dark room illuminated just by the parting of the curtain and the silver ray of the moon that streams through it. The lump on the bed doesn't move. Everything is still, and I feel bad for disturbing the silence, my footsteps on the thick carpet bringing me nearer to the platform. Standing above the sleeping form, I pause.

Soren looks precisely the same as the last time I saw him. The dark veins that were visible under his pale skin are gone, making his eternally youthful face exquisite and too perfect to be real. His platinum hair spreads out on the pillow like a cloud around his face, where the silver light of the moon creates shadows. My stomach clenches at seeing them dance around him.

"I have questions." Chewing on the inside of my mouth, I think on how to approach this.

Nothing. Not even a flutter of his thick eyelashes.

"You can't pretend to sleep while people are dying, Soren." Clenching and unclenching my fists, I loom over him. "Not even you can be that selfish."

Nope. Nothing.

"You gave me that dumb speech of sacrifices, on how you are here willingly because you believe in destinies and fates, yet here you are." Pacing in front of the bed, I wave my hands, agitated. "Sleeping away while those you claim to be protecting are dying left and right." Stopping above his head, I stab a finger in his face. "You are a liar!"

Nada. Not even a change in his breathing.

All the fight leaves me in a rush. I drop next to the bed, crawling closer and leaning on it. Pressing the back of my head to the soft covers, I stare at the ceiling, sadness pulling me down like an anvil is tied around my ankles. Even when my life went to shit, I stupidly thought I'd at least be able to save the rest of Sienna. No more innocent people will die. The joke is on me. Fat tears trickle out of the corners of my eyes, soaking my hair and the covers I'm resting on.

"I came here with a dagger ready to stab you if you don't talk to me." Hiccupping a cough that sounds a lot like a sob, I shake my head at myself. "I can't even do that right."

Tears keep rolling down my cheeks in rivulets. Angrily, I swipe at them with the back of my hand. They keep coming, so eventually I give up, my chest shaking in silent sobs.

"You have so much life, so much passion in you, child." Soren's rasp has me spinning fast to make sure I am not imagining it.

"Now you want to fucking talk?" Laughing like a crazy person, I wipe the tears with my forearm. "It was mentioning the dagger that woke your old ass up, wasn't it?"

"I always know when you are here." He chuckles.

"That's all sorts of wrong, you know that, right? And rude!" Now that I know he really is awake and I'm not insane, I plop back down as I was before with my head on the bed. "Rude old fart, that's what you are. Why don't you say something? At least tell me to get the hell out."

"I have nothing to say." He sounds thoughtful. "When I do, I speak. And I like it when you come to see me."

"So, you have something to say now?" I perk up at that. Maybe he will tell me something useful for once.

"No." He sounds as confused as I feel.

"You know that you are talking now."

"You were crying." I can hear him move his head in my direction.

"So that's the trick to get you talking? All I have to do is cry?" Incredulous, I turn to glare at him.

"I don't like it when you are crying, child." Sighing, he shifts on the bed. "We are the same, you and I. We feel too much. It's a hard burden to bear."

Fear stabs me at his words. Is this what I have to look forward to? To sleep forever, waking up only when I have something to say? There must be another way. Maybe fighting the hunters is not that bad of a thing after all. Which reminds me why I'm here.

"You know that someone is killing off guards and students here?" Pressing my forearms on the bed, and climbing to my knees, it's like I'm praying to him. Or for him. "You—" Rethinking my words, I rephrase what I wanted to say. "We are connected, bonded to the academy. I'm still new to this and don't understand it. Do you know who is doing this? Who is killing between these walls?"

"There are always those that try to hurt this academy." With his eyes still closed, he shifts again. "There will always be those that will try to hurt it."

"Okay." Dragging out the word, I wait. "That's it? That's all you've got?"

"What is your question, child."

"Do you or do you not know who is killing in this

place?" Pushing the words through clenched teeth, I glower at his peaceful face.

"That is the wrong question," he tells me gently, and I see red.

"I don't fucking know how to ask the question, Soren. People are dying, I want to stop whoever is killing them. Phrase that as the best version of a question on your own."

"You are angry with me." He sounds like freaking Zoltan right now. "I do wish to help you; I just don't know what you need from me."

"If you keep pissing me off, I'm going to come one day and dress you in a tutu. A pink one with glitter on it."

"What's a tutu?" Soren sounds genuinely curious, and I find myself answering him.

"A fluffy skirt." Snorting at how ridiculous that sounds, I blow out a breath. "I'll dress you up in a skirt."

"Ah." He chuckles happily.

"You like wearing skirts?" I eye him to see if he will tell the truth.

"I do not know." A big smile stretches his lips. "I've never worn one. This tutu you are talking about."

"Tell me how to stop this killer and I'll buy you one in every color." I think I realize that Soren is like a child. Things that stress us out mean nothing to him at all.

"With glitter?" Is that excitement in his voice? What the hell?

"You like glitter?' I flinch at the way I ask that question. I'm no one to judge what he likes or doesn't like.

"I do like things that sparkle." A grin stretches his lips.

"Fine, I'll start bringing you shiny things if you help me out." If this doesn't work, I'm fresh out of ideas.

"No one kills for no reason." All the happiness and humor leave his face. "Those that do for the sake of taking a life are messy, gruesome killings. Was that what you found between our walls?"

"It's not messy, no. The bodies are just left there, all the blood missing." A shiver rakes my spine. "The ones in Sienna, it's that shadow. The one consuming them all." Argoz didn't say that, but I have no doubt in my mind I'm right.

Soren's eyes snap open.

"Shadow? Consuming life?" The yellow dragon eyes search my face. I hold my breath, forgetting how to speak for a second.

My head jerks in fast nods.

"Yes, it's horrifying, Soren." Gulping air, I blow it out a couple of times to calm down. "I've never felt so terrified in my life."

"You have seen it?"

"Yes, once." Recalling that night, I remember the male that saved me. Zoltan. My heart thumps painfully in my chest. "Zoltan saved me, although I didn't know who he was at the time."

"Yes, Zoltan has many strengths. One good thing this academy has done." Soren nods thoughtfully. "The shadow you speak of that devours life sounds like one of the old gods. None of them have crossed a portal. This I know."

"I know what I saw."

"Be that as it may, magic is a powerful force for those who know how to wield it. Perhaps your answers lie there." His eyelashes flutter, and his eyes close. "Speaking is so tiring at times."

Knowing I'm out of time and won't get much more out of him, my words come out in a rush. "And the one killing here? Tell me something, anything. Please." My hand latches onto his arm over the covers.

"Blood." His lips barely move as he mumbles. "The answer is always in the blood, child. And it has nothing to do with family." With that enigmatic comment, he smiles and goes silent.

"Grcat!" Plopping back down, I huff a breath. "Like we need more riddles."

My thoughts are racing, trying to decipher what his words mean. Do we need to look for the blood that's missing from the bodies? Excitement claws at me. Was I right and Cassius is somehow related to that hunter Jack? Are all the answers with his daughter? Maybe she is our killer; she sure had a nasty attitude. But he did say it has nothing to do with family. What the fuck does that mean?

My eyes get heavy, and I slump more on the thick carpet. I can feel my body sliding to the side and the soft fibers pressing on my cheek. I know I should get up and go find my room, but I'll just stay here for a moment. Just to think everything through. My last thought is, *I hope there will be no new body to find tomorrow.*

Chapter Twenty-One

"You really love stressing the life out of everyone." Fenrir's frustrated growl meets me the second I step foot out of the golden hallway.

I did feel bad when I opened my eyes and realized I'd fallen asleep next to Soren's bed like a pet that didn't want to leave his side. It didn't last long—the guilt I mean. I can't remember the last time I've been this rested. Soren might be an annoying and selfish old fart, but there is something about him and his presence that gives me peace. The similarities we share might be it. I'm not sure and I don't care. I feel like I can take on the world right now.

"Right, because I did this on purpose." Pushing the sleeves up my forearms, my shoulder bumps into him when I pass him by. "Do you have any news, or did you just stand here to tell me what a horrible person I am for falling asleep?"

"How are you feeling?" The Fae falls into step with me, and the worry in his musical voice makes me feel like shit for snapping at him.

"Like I was never hurt, if that's what you're asking." Blowing out a breath, I shove my hands in the pockets of the pants. "That mage you have on call is excellent. Maybe you should be nicer to him."

"That's good. You are handling it better than most." Ignoring my not-so-subtle comment about the mage, Fenrir sighs in relief. "Not that it surprises me."

"Is Astara not doing well?"

I call Soren selfish, yet I haven't even thought about my friend. And I say I hate hypocrites. *Reality check, Franky,* the voice chirps in my head. I push it down in frustration; the last thing I need is to have conversations in my mind with the multiple personalities sharing this body.

"She needed to rest and feed." Fenrir waves away my worries with a flick of his wrist. "She will be fine … is fine, I promise," he adds when I suck in a sharp breath.

"Where is she?" My feet are already moving faster as I lift my nose in the air, sniffing in hopes of catching her scent. "And no one died in the meantime, right? Because if someone did, that should've been the first thing coming out of your mouth."

"No one died." He chuckles. "Leo and his pack were on watch ever since you left to see Soren. Did he talk to you?"

"You're getting off track. Astara?"

"She took your room for the night. I think she was expecting you to be there after seeing Soren. I assume she's still there."

"That's perfect." When he lifts an eyebrow at me, I shake my head. "I need a shower and to get out of these clothes. Two birds, one stone and all that."

"Ah, right. Well, I just wanted to see that you are well." Nodding thoughtfully, he scans the open space around us, his head tilting up to check the winding stairways, as well. "I have a few things I need to check, Zoltan and Argoz are looking into Cassius's daughter and his bloodline. When you freshen up, you and Astara can meet us in the dining hall."

'What, no more talks behind closed doors?" I have no idea why I'm doing my best to irritate him. It's not his fault any of this is happening.

"We all need to eat." Not taking the bait, Fenrir gives me a smile and a curt nod, veering off to one of the hallways.

I slow down, watching him walk away. We have come a long way—all of us—in such a short time. For some reason, I think about all the years I spent as part of the Supernatural Agency of the Accord, and how unwelcome and tense I felt the whole time there. Even my partner—including the couple I had before him—made me feel like I didn't belong there. I was never enough. Not smart enough, not fast or strong enough. How strange that I feel so accepted in the one place that should want me dead.

Soren's words echo in my head. *"The answer is always in the blood, child. And it has nothing to do with family."* Can it be that simple? Was everyone purposely misled to believe that half-bloods are despised and unwelcomed, as well as killed on sight by Daywalker Academy and its residents for merely being hybrids? Or is there more to it?

Shaking off that never-ending train of thought, I rub my forearms, warding off the sudden chill I feel. My skin prickles, goosebumps spreading up my arms and legs. With a frown, I swivel my head, searching for something or someone. People move around with their heads bowed, the silence stretching around, only the clicks of their boots on the tiled floors creating a rhythm that matches the beat of my heart. They are not looking at each other, and the familiar hum of hushed conversations or the occasional laugh or shout I come to expect is missing. Passing the stairways with my gaze, I do a double take when my brain registers a familiar face climbing up to the third floor, but it's gone before I blink.

"You are seeing shit, Franky. Go shower. You stink." Reprimanding myself under my breath, I spin on my heel, heading to my room.

The hallways change from the nicely-decorated ones with plush runners adorning the floors to the stark gray I'm accustomed to. I do slow down for a moment when I walk by the portraits hanging in one of them—one in particular luring my eyes to pay it attention. I still can't figure out why it nags at me that I should know who it is. I do have to turn around after that since I forget the Fae, and the bloodsucker made me change rooms. That's my life now, I guess. They move me around whenever they feel like it.

Reaching my door, I shove it open. "Honey, I'm home!"

"It's about time," Astara drawls, stretching out on the bed and leaning her head in her hand after she props up on an elbow. "It made me realize how boring it is without you around."

"What can I say? I'm here for your entertainment." Giving her a grin, I push the door closed. "You feeling okay?"

"As good as new." She grins back but sobers up fast. "I didn't get a chance to say thank you."

"You should thank Fenrir, not me. And try not to make it seem like you are really, really, thankful. He is arrogant enough already." My attempt to turn it into a joke is wasted.

"I heard what you said." She swings her legs around, sitting up on the bed. "Whoever doesn't see what a wonderful person you are is an idiot." I shuffle my feet, feeling uncomfortable under her pinning gaze. "I'm the one that should be grateful you call me your friend."

"Grateful. Friend. Right. Okay." Groaning because I know I sound like an idiot, I stab my fingers in my hair, scratching at my skull. "I'm not good with mushy stuff. Sorry. Thank you?"

"You don't have to say anything." She laughs at the pained look on my face, and probably for phrasing the words "thank you" as a question. "Let's just not talk about it and rock the shit out of this friendship. What say you?"

"I can do that." With a smile stretching my lips, I duck my head to hide the reddening of my cheeks. "Right after I shower." Catching a whiff of the dried blood and sweat makes me gag.

"Yea!" Waving a hand like she's shooing me off, she wrinkles her nose. "Go wash, you stinking peasant." Her laughter follows me in the bathroom. "And leave the door open so I can talk to you. I won't perv, I promise."

The smile stays on my face as I yank the clothes off me in disgust. The fabric has gone so stiff at this point that it looks like I'm still wearing them even when I take them off. *Never do this again, Franky.* Breathing through my mouth, I agree with that completely.

"At least we had an uneventful time while you were with Soren," Astara calls out.

"I thought you were resting." Sticking my head out, I scowl at her.

"I rested, fed, and then wanted to check on things. What with guards dying around and all that." Her mouth twists in a grimace. "Better be safe than sorry."

"It had nothing to do with one particular guard, I'm sure." Ducking back in the bathroom, I squeal—actually squeal when she throws a pillow at my head.

"Whatever." I peek again, but her glare sends me to the shower. "What I'm saying is everything was normal. Not even the usual sneaking out of rooms happened, apparently."

Stepping under the spray of water feels like I'm being reborn. Astara stays quiet while I watch all the dirt and grime swirl at my feet, disappearing down the drain. My mind wants to drift to many important things pushing for attention, but I force everything down, allowing myself to just breathe. But right now, I feel like this is the calm before the storm, and no matter how hard I try, I can't get the feeling to go away.

I feel Zoltan somewhere nearby, not close enough to be in my room, but close enough. My heart picks up a beat, and just this once, I let it. Soren said the Daywalker is one thing this academy has done right. I have to agree with that. I'll be damned if I become his downfall. Washing my hair roughly, frustration digging a hole in my chest, I push the thoughts of him away, too.

When the water runs clear, I step out of the shower, snatching a towel off the hook sticking from the wall. I stare at my reflection in the foggy mirror, my hand swiping a line where I can clearly see my face. The water is gathered on my eyelashes, turning them into a few thicker peeks sticking out of my eyelids. Droplets trickle on the sides of my face, stopping for a moment at my chin and clinging for dear life before they fall, splattering on my collarbone. That's how I feel right now. Like I'm holding onto a cliff, nails digging in solid rock but slipping with each breath I take. Eventually, I'll lose my grip and splatter like the droplets of water falling from my face.

The magic pulses in the center of my chest.

Shaking the thoughts away, I take a deep breath, my

vision clearing. A slight smile lifts the corners of my lips while I dry myself. It is almost as if the magic is trying to comfort me. Reminding me that there are things I still don't understand that maybe, just maybe, will be enough to keep me on that cliff. If not forever, at least long enough.

"Fenrir said to meet them in the dining hall when we are ready." Stepping out with the towel wrapped around me, I rummage through the drawers to look for clothes.

"Sounds like a good plan. I'm starving." A loud growl from my stomach follows her words, and she laughs. "I'm not the only one it seems."

"I can't remember the last time I ate." Pressing a hand to my stomach, I rush back in the bathroom, dressing up as fast as I can.

"Oh, I don't know," Astara chirps. "I seem to remember clearly the last time you fed yourself."

"Oh, dear fates, don't be an ass." All the blood rushes to my face, my cheeks burning. "Don't ever mention that." Coming out, I stab my feet in some boots. "Like, ever."

"I'm just saying." She shrugs, and I wonder if her face hurts from her lips stretching so wide.

"That's what I get for having a friend." Grumbling, I buckle the boots but can't stop my smile. "Let's go see what the males have to say for themselves."

"I can't wait to hear what Soren said." Jumping off the bed, she's first out the door. "Curiosity has been eating me alive, but I kept my mouth shut."

"Curiosity killed the cat"—Following behind her, I close and lock the room—"or so they say."

"Not this cat, I assure you." Clawing the air in my face, she grins evilly. "This cat has very sharp claws."

"And fangs." Laughing when she lifts her chin proudly, I push her gently. "Let's not forget the fangs. Now, move."

Chapter Twenty-Two

The air is literally sucked out of the room the moment I step foot in the dining hall. Astara stiffens next to me but otherwise stays quiet. It's not as packed as it usually is, which makes me wonder if people chose to stay in their rooms—or anywhere else they need to be—to not risk being exposed to our killer. I always think there is safety in numbers, but what do I know? Being alone is my choice rather than having people around me because I can always count on myself.

My passing gaze sweeps the space before landing on the usual spot we call our own. I know Fenrir, Argoz, and Leo are there, but my focus stays on the pair of blue eyes that hold me hostage no matter where I am. Casually leaning on the arm of his chair, Zoltan tracks me like the predator that he is. My entire body comes alive.

"It's all her fucking fault." The not-too-quiet growl reaches my ears when we pass a table with two males sitting alone. The one shooting daggers at me through his eyes is the one that has spoken, I guess.

"People were dying in Sienna before I stepped foot here, asshole." Clenching my fist, I stop, looming over him. "Your portals were being attacked, as well. How exactly is it my fault? Or do you have no one else to blame?"

His eyes widen. Apparently, he didn't expect me to reply. The color in them swirls, his animal rearing its head up, reacting to the aggression in my voice. With his bulky frame, my guess is he's a feline shifter.

"Let's go, Franky." Astara pulls me by the arm, and I let her lead me away.

The hush is thicker now.

I'm surprised that the males are still in their seats, watching but not interfering. They haven't moved a muscle, looking as relaxed as they can be. My heart is beating a staccato in my chest, and I wipe my sweaty palms on my thighs as subtly as I can. Zoltan locks his gaze on the movement. Nothing escapes him.

"Food!" Astara rushes when we near them, grabbing a plate and bouncing next to Fenrir on the sofa.

"She is starving." My explanation is met with silence and more staring. "Annddd, here we are." Lowering myself onto the chair they left empty for me, I reach for my own plate so I can avoid their gazes.

"You should've said something." Astara talks over a mouthful of pastry at Zoltan.

"She handled it." I feel his eyes boring into the top of my head while I stare at the food on my plate.

"Yes," Fenrir snorts ungracefully. "Just like she handles everything else. Like an elephant in a glass house." My head snaps up, and he grins at me.

"Ms. Drake has … her talents," Argoz pipes in helpfully.

I glare at him.

"Can we not talk about me right now?" Waving a hand

to encompass the room, I frown at all of them. "I would think we have more important things to talk about."

"Yes, we do." The Fae sniffs, the arrogant ass. "Let's hear what Soren said. He hasn't spoken to the Board at all, even when they told him about the killings."

"He already knew about that?" Pushing the words through clenched teeth, the plate cracks under my grip when I imagine it's Soren's neck I'm squeezing. "I really should've stabbed him."

Argoz sucks in a sharp breath, looking petrified.

"I didn't." Drawling at his reaction, I can't hold back the grimace I make.

Zoltan's lips quirk at the corners.

"Francesca." The reprimand in Fenrir's voice is enough to make me deflate.

"It took some doing, but he did wake up." Blowing out a breath, I sagged in the chair, placing the cracked plate on my thighs. I look at Zoltan. "He said the shadows that are attacking the people in Sienna sound like one of the old gods, but that none have gone through the portals."

"Impossible." Argoz almost jumps from where he is sitting. The tension in the air presses on my shoulders, pushing me deeper in the chair. "There must be a mistake."

"Well, possible or not, that's what he said. I also told him that I know what I saw." My knee starts bouncing, jostling the plate in my lap, so I move it on the table. "The answer I got was: magic can be powerful in the hands of those who know how to wield it. Bringing us back to the mages."

A look passes between Fenrir and Zoltan.

"Well, do share with the rest of us." Nails digging in the armrests, I wiggle in the chair. "That's why we're here."

"There is a possibility that Cassius is behind the potion

the hunters are using." Fenrir sounds pained to admit it. "A couple of old tomes are missing from the library. All with spells and potions that haven't been used for centuries."

"You have shit like that just sitting around here for anyone to take?" My jaw unhinges at that information, and I gape at them. "Really?"

"Cassius was not everyone." The ghoul sounds insulted. "Not everyone has access to everything."

"Obviously." My voice is so dry I see dust coming out of my mouth.

"We are getting off track," Leo finally speaks, leaning his forearms on his spread-out thighs. "What else did Soren say?"

"I asked about the killings of the guards and students." Pursing my lips, I flick my gaze at all of them. "After giving me a lecture that there are always those that want to attack the academy, he gave me a riddle. The answer is always in the blood." I watch them all like a hawk, hoping for a reaction. They all stare blankly back. "And it has nothing to do with family."

"You think Franky is onto something with this hunter looking like Cassius's daughter?" Astara turns to her brother, a line forming between her eyebrows.

"Could be." Zoltan looks thoughtful.

"That's not exactly nothing to do with family." Pointing out the obvious, I place a hand on top of my knee to stop it from bouncing. "It's the opposite."

"We've been keeping an eye on her since we got back," Leo growls in frustration, and my heart sinks. "She hasn't moved from her room, apart from a couple of classes and the library."

"The same library that has books with shit that can kill

us?" My voice sounds accusing, but I don't care. Protecting their egos is not my problem.

"She took History books." Leo's words are emotionless.

"So, we are back to square one." Huffing a breath, I grab my hair in both hands. "There must be something we are missing. There must be." I look at them with desperation.

"We will find them, Franky." Astara makes an effort to sound convincing but fails. She looks as desperate as I do.

"I guess I wasn't invited to this get together. I'm insulted," a deep voice like rolling rocks down a hill says from behind me.

I whirl around, almost falling off the chair to stare at Alex. Standing right behind my chair, in black leather from head to toe, he looms over me. His lips are lifted in a smile, but those eyes watch me like he can see through me. My skin pebbles, a shiver crawling up my spine at something I can't name. His power barely touches mine, like he is holding back so no one can notice what he is doing.

"Alex." Zoltan's voice can cut through stone. "Come join us."

"Why, thank you," Walking around, he plops down next to Azgor, his knee grazing mine when he sits. "I would love to."

Argoz says something I don't hear. The others join in the conversation, but everything is just white noise floating past my ears. Astara gives me a strange look, but I ignore her, focusing on Alex like he will disappear if I blink. I watch him talk about something, his head tilting back when he laughs.

"When did you come here?" My question is barely air passing my lips, but all conversation stops like someone presses mute on the remote control.

"Should I have asked permission to visit my academy, Ms. Drake?" he says mockingly, arching an eyebrow at me.

"When"—Stretching the words slowly in case he is dumb to understand them, I lean forward—"did you come here?"

"Shortly after you left," Argoz rushes to answer, leaving Alex with his mouth open and a frustrated look on his face.

"While we were fighting hunters in your building, you came here?" The magic in my chest stirs at the look flashing in his eyes.

"You brought hunters to my door. Roberti is hell bent on getting his hands on you." Alex's face twists in a rage-filled mask. "You will forgive me for coming to check on my mate, half blood."

"When did the killings happen?" Ignoring the insult, I turn to the ghoul.

Something Alex said nags at me, but I find my question more important. My eyes flick to Argoz, who is watching me with eyes so wide they're about to pop out of his skull and roll on the table. His head swivels from me to Alex.

"Shortly after you left for the human world." The ghoul gulps, and power slams into me from Zoltan and Fenrir like a truck.

"Around the time he came?" My body stiffens, preparing for the fight that's coming. I can feel it in my bones.

"I-I sup-I suppose," Argoz stutters and all hell breaks loose.

Everyone jumps just a second too late. Something prickles my thigh, and all the strength leaves my body, making me slump in the chair. I see Alex dropping the syringe from his hand, grabbing me at the same time. Everything blurs when I'm thrown over a shoulder, the bone digging in my stomach while Alex runs out of the dining hall faster than anyone I've ever seen. Zoltan's rage-filled roar shatters the windows we are passing, shards of glass sinking in my skin like tiny needles. Alex stumbles when a loud boom rocks the ground under his feet, the earsplitting wails of a siren making my eyes cross in pain.

The portal.

We are being attacked right now while I flop uselessly over this asshole's shoulder, and there is nothing I can do. There is no mistaking the warning when the portal is under attack, the blood dripping from my ears reminding me of my first day here. Only this time, it's not Zoltan carrying me around gently in his arms.

This time a killer has me in his clutches.

The vibrations on my thighs where he holds them pressed to his chest tell me he is saying something. Cursing me to hell probably. I can feel Zoltan getting closer, and that gives me some relief. Not that he will save me. I have no idea what Alex had in that syringe, but whatever it is, it's burning through my veins so painfully I can't even summon the strength to scream. But Zoltan will kill the fucker. I have no doubt about that.

I know the exact moment Alex is outside of the academy building. My blood drips and splatters on the soil, the magic of this place, that ancient monstrosity that is a part of me now surges up, answering the call of the pulse in my chest. I'm thrown on the ground not far from the portal when the earth shutters violently, sending Alex sprawling on the opposite side.

I can see his ugly, twisted face turning my way through the strands of hair falling all over my face. I grin. Or I try to anyway, and his scowl deepens. Pounding footsteps echo under my ear that's pressed in the soil, the loudest of them all, like the hill itself is rushing to my aid, are Zoltan's. I know it's him by the way the weight of his body is placed on the balls of his feet. Who knew I paid that much attention to the vampire?

Alex yanks me up like a lifeless puppet by the arm. My legs scrape the ground from the knee down, the tips of my boots bumping every tiny rock littering the floor. He drags me towards the swirling portal, my head rolling on my shoulders.

Another pulse of the ancient magic hits me at the center of my chest, my body convulsing like someone sticks a high voltage wire in my heart. Alex is thrown away from me, the blast sending his feet inside the portal while his body is stretched on our side. Just as the sky opens and a torrent of rain pours on us like from an open faucet, Zoltan's boots stop in my vision. Raindrops jump and dance on top of his boots, reminding me of fairies dancing, just like the first time I saw him.

White boots step out through the portal.

Chapter Twenty-Three

Fenrir joins Zoltan, both of them standing with their legs spread shoulder-width apart like a living shield in front of me. My body is still convulsing, flopping like a fish out of water. Astara drops on her knees next to me, giving a futile attempt to help me. She is thrown away, as well. I keep my terrified gaze on the portal as one by one hunters pass through it, spreading out like a virus through these lands. The magic in the ground is rebelling from it.

Shifter and demon guards rush to help, spreading like the sea to block further access. The feeling in my body slowly returns, and along with it comes the sound. Shouts and roars split the night, even the moon hanging low in the sky pulsing in anger. They shouldn't be here. With shaking fingers, I lift on my hands and knees, still trembling from the shocks of magic cursing through my veins.

"How is this for magic, Soren." My numb lips tingle as they graze the dirt under my palms.

"Francesca?" Zoltan's voice is part worry, part question.

"Hellion, you okay?" Fenrir pirouettes in front of me,

catching a dagger in the air and sending it back to where it came from. His hair flies around his head, exposing his pointed ears.

He should show those ears more often, I think in my delirium, racked with pain.

"I'm great, Fae." Grinding my teeth, I'm finally able to sit up on my knees. "How are you this evening?"

"She'll be fine," he tells Zoltan like the vampire can't hear me. "If she can be a smartass, she is fine."

Zoltan crouches in front of me, pushing the hair sticking to my face behind my ears. His thumb rubs off the blood that is dripping there, glaring at it like the drops of blood are at fault for daring to come out of my body. A crazed laugh shakes my shoulders, making him look at my face. All around us people are fighting.

"Sorry I was bleeding." Chuckling, I push his hands away. "It won't happen again."

"It better not, Ms. Drake." He smirks, taking the sting out of calling me that.

"How is this possible?" The humor drains out of me. "I thought they couldn't get through the portals."

"They shouldn't be able to." Zoltan turns his head, his gaze locking on something to my right. "Unless someone gave them access."

Following his line of sight, I see Alex fighting a shifter, his large hands gripping the puma and ripping the head off. Blood sprays in an arch in the air like a thrown bucket of paint. My stomach clenches when the shifter's body drops on the ground.

"He knows how to break the wards?" Rubbing the back of my hand, I try to wipe the blood I can feel wetting my upper lip.

Zoltan takes that hand, his thumb smearing the blood. "He knew he needed a dragon blood to pass through."

"He set us up." Remembering that I bled all over his building, I want to scream. "We should've known as soon as he mentioned Roberti."

"He was always treading a thin line, but never like this," Fenrir growls, still twisting and turning to protect us. "Unless …"

"Unless what?" I finally stand up, feeling that I'm not about to topple over. Zoltan hovers his arm just in case, and I slap it away.

"Unless they want to tear the portal exposing Sienna to the human world." The Fae grunts, punching a hunter that has the dumb idea to get close enough.

"It'll be a slaughter"—Fear claws like sharp talons at my chest—"on both sides."

"I think that's the idea." Zoltan grinds his teeth so hard I can hear them in my head like nails on a chalkboard.

I release the hold I have on the pulsing magic inside me, seeing the bright swirling colors of the darkness coming to life between one blink and the next. I know my eyes have changed as well because the thin veins under Zoltan's skin branch out like small rivers over his features. He is still breathtaking.

"Let's go kick their ass." Fenrir startles, giving me a strange look over his shoulder. "A perk for being a freak." I wave my hand around my face in explanation.

With a sharp nod, Zoltan is gone, disappearing in the throngs of people fighting. With one last look at Fenrir's back, I turn on my heel, heading for the first hunter I see. The idiots are dressed all in white, quickly picked. They should rethink their dress policy, I think, but who am I to complain? They make my job easy.

My feet barely touch the ground as I sprint, jumping and twisting midair at the hunter. His eyes bulge out of his face a second before I twist his head, ripping it off. The demon that is fighting him grunts in acknowledgment before running to find another opponent. I weave through it all, kicking, punching and ripping throats, blood dripping down my chin and soaking my shirt. *I just had a shower.* The thought makes me laugh. Maybe I am insane.

I see Leo—his wolf towering over everyone else—being cornered by three hunters, their short swords hacking the air around his legs. The shifter is nimble for such a large animal, his paws dancing out of the way just in time. Saliva is dripping from his deadly-sharp jaws. Turning his way, I plow through two of the hunters, sending them face first on the forest floor. Grabbing one by the hair, I yank his head back, the crunch of his neck braking grating my teeth. Leo swoops in, ripping his throat out.

Spinning around, I throw the head I'm clutching by the hair at the hunter that remains standing. It hits him at the center of his chest, the blood splattering over his white shirt. The last thing he sees is fangs poking under my upper lip when I grin at him, ripping his neck open. He drops at my feet.

A pull has me turning my head, my gaze finding Zoltan. He is far from me, but I see him clearly, carving a way through wave after wave of hunters. There is a low wall around him made of dead bodies, their number growing with each move of his arms. Face set in determination, he looks like a dark angel claiming death as his due.

A pained roar jerks my head behind me. I see the shifter from the dining hall—the one blaming me for all this— clutching his abdomen, stumbling away from two hunters. They move fast, but not as quickly as me. I'm before them with the shifter at my back between one breath and the next. Both of them stop their advance, spreading wider apart from each other. Long, silver blades glint in the moonlight when they twirl them around, looking for an opening.

"Oh, how sweet. You brought big pointy sticks." I grin at them, and they take a step back. "I'm already scared."

The hunter on my right swings at me, his sword raising high and coming down in an arch at my head. Bending back, I watch the silver weapon pass in front of my eyes, not even an inch from my nose. My skin prickles from the air being cut so close. Coming back up, I spin, kicking him in his gut and sending him flying back into the trees. His body hits with a sickening crunch, dropping on the floor and not getting back up.

I twirl away from the second blade that catches the fabric of my shirt, tearing it open and exposing the bottom of my breasts. Dropping on the floor, I spin around and stretch one leg out, sweeping the feet from under the hunter. He collapses on his back with a grunt, and I pounce on him, my knees digging hard into his chest. Remembering what everyone told me about the covers on their faces, I grab hold of it, yanking as hard as I can.

His head separates from his body, the fabric still attached to his face. With a disgusted grimace, I throw it away, standing up. The shifter stares at me like he's never seen me before. I expect fear or revulsion, but only curiosity sparkles in his feline eyes.

"You're welcome." Everything else I am going to say leaves my thoughts when I hear Astara's outraged cry.

I'm sprinting in the direction of her voice before I even fully turn. My heart is in my throat, the dark blotches where the still-fighting hunters are dirtying the pulsing bright colors blurring my sight. I stop dead in my tracks when I see that she is not hurt.

It's much worse.

Zoltan stands stock still, fists clenched, and a muscle jumping angrily on his chiseled jaw. Alex and Cassius flank him on either side, both holding daggers dripping with black potion under his chin. His entire body is vibrating in rage, but he doesn't move. When I see Cassius's daughter standing right behind them with a hand pressed on Alex's back, everything becomes clear. All the fighting has stopped, everyone staring at the entrance of the portal. A hunter thrusts his blade at my chest, but I spin, grabbing his arm and wrenching it out of his socket. The hunter screams a bloodcurdling sound when his arm dangles in my hand. I drop it at my feet, my eyes never leaving Zoltan's.

"I knew you had it in you, Franky." I recoil from Andrius's voice a second before he steps through the portal.

Dark energy comes off him in waves, darkness dancing like a living cloak around his shoulders. Moving closer to where they hold Zoltan, his gaze traces my body slowly up and down, lingering on the exposed glimpse of my breasts. Bile rises in the back of my throat.

Another hunter inches closer from my side and my arm shoots out, my fingers gripping his throat and my nails digging in his windpipe. My hand curls, sinking into flesh, blood drenching it to my wrist. I open my fingers, releasing the blob in my hand to follow the crumbling body of the gurgling hunter to the ground.

"She is magnificent." Andrius claps his hands in glee, his eyes glittering with madness. "Isn't she?"

"It's me you want, Roberti." Taking a step closer, I ignore Zoltan's glare. "Let him go."

"Why should I do that?" He sounds like we are

discussing the price of potatoes at the market. Anger bubbles in my chest. "When I can have you both?"

"You'll have a lot of dead hunters and might even lose your useless life if you don't let him go." Sliding my feet on the floor, I inch closer. "If you think I'll come willingly after you hurt him, you are crazier than I thought."

"I won't hurt him." Andrius, in his right mind, slaps Zoltan's face good-naturedly. My chest vibrates from the vampire's growl. "He is leverage."

"Why are you doing this?" I think I see Leo's tail slinking on the side, but I can't be sure. I slide closer. "What is it you want?"

"It's not what I want, Drake." His face twists in anger. "It's what everyone wants. Don't you see?" Spreading his arm around, he points at the people around us. "Who decided that vampires are the top of the food chain, that the rest of us should crawl at their feet? You think the shifters and the demons don't loathe being guards. Being treated like the dirt under their shoe. Well"—He grins with no humor—"let's see them now. There is a bigger power in town."

"That's it? You are doing this for your ego, you stupid fuck?" I see a hunter inching closer from the corner of my eye, but I'm too angry to care. "You are killing innocents in Sienna, and in the academy, so you can feel important. You really are a moron, you know that, right?"

"You'll see things my way soon enough, Drake," Andrius snarls. "Now get your ass through the portal, or it'll go down. Alex was smart enough to get enough of your blood to bring all the portals down. Let's see how you feel knowing it's you that is responsible for so many deaths."

"You will not pin this on me." But his words stab me in

the chest. What the shifter said to me in the dining room ringing in my ears. "It's all her fault."

"Don't listen to him." Fenrir materializes next to me, his power holding by a thin thread, ready to explode and knock us all over. "He is full of shit."

"Should I kill him now, and we fight?" Andrius leans forward in anticipation. "What do you say, Fenrir? With Zoltan dead, you can have her all to yourself." He leers at me, making my skin crawl.

"He won't kill him," a woman's voice hisses to my right and I stiffen when I catch a glimpse of white clothing. "He s bluffing, don't be stupid. Let him take him; you can get him out." It sounds so familiar it takes a moment to place it.

"What the fuck?" hissing under my breath, I'm grateful Andrius is focused on the Fae at the moment. "Myst?"

"I got you, chica. That asshat manipulated me, as well. I knew Alex was up to something." She inches closer, raising all the red flags in my head. Fenrir says something I don't hear.

"And I should trust you, why?" Everything is so messed up right now I want to scream until my throat is raw.

"You shouldn't." She snickers like a nutcase. "But the enemy of my enemy is my friend. He won't kill the hunk. But he can bring the portals down."

"Fuck me." I breathe and she snorts.

"You're hot and all, but I don't swing that way." When Fenrir fidgets next to me, I know he can hear us and that my time is up.

"What will it be, Drake?" Andrius glows in glee. "The Daywalker or Sienna?"

All eyes turn on me. I feel their gazes like hands grabbing at me, pulling me down a never-ending abyss of torment. My eyes lock on Astara's, my friend begging silently for me to save her brother. Everything I am shatters into tiny pieces. I die inside as I still breathe. That crazy bitch better pray she tells the truth.

"I choose Sienna, you crazy motherfucker."

Pushing off the floor with both feet, I sail through the air with everything I have, aiming for Zoltan. My arms are outstretched, and I can almost feel the fabric of his shirt under my skin. They pull him through the portal just as the fighting starts again. I drop on my knees. He let them take him with a proud smile on his handsome face.

Astara's scream rips my heart out.

Next in the Daywalker Series

vinci-books.com/instigated

Blood can betray you—but it never lies.

The portals are cracked, the gods are stirring, and I'm done being anyone's pawn. If I want to save the one person who matters, I'll have to burn it all down.

Good thing chaos runs in my blood.

Turn the page for a free preview…

Instigated: Chapter One

My nails dig into the mortar between the bricks where I'm clinging for dear life, making my fingers ache. The tips of my boots scrape between bricks, searching for purchase just as a fat drop of rain splatters on the tip of my nose on my upturned face, spraying my eyes. Blinking fast to clear my vision, I finally find one brick protruding from the others, letting the tip of the boot rest there as I press my face to the wall.

"This was a very dumb idea." Huffing under my breath, I try to slow my breathing.

I'm suspended two stories up on the outside of the academy building, hanging for all to see like an idiot. I'm counting on no one looking up, but if I don't move fast I'll eventually be spotted. My arms and legs burn from the effort it takes me to crawl up like a spider in the middle of the night. Hopefully it'll pay off, if my guess is right. With one last slow breath, my heart galloping in my chest, I continue the laborious climb. I've seen humans doing this for fun on TV. Rock climbing they call it, the idiots. Who would do this for fun?

Sweat trickles from between my shoulder blades down my spine by the time I see the curving rooftiles within reach. I can't feel my fingers anymore, and my muscles scream in pain all over my body. Maybe I should do more than just the calming yoga exercises I've been sticking with the last couple of years. I almost laugh at the thought, but I'm too tired. Running for your life is exercise enough, right?

Summoning all the energy I have left, I swing my lower body like a pendulum, arms shaking from the weight as I fling one leg over the edge of the rooftiles. Everything around me swims, dizziness making me lightheaded when I end up hanging with my head down, my braid like a rope tapping the wall. Wedging my foot between the tile and a pipe, I pull my other leg up and finally plop on my back.

Another fat drop of rain splatters my cheek.

Keeping my eyes closed, I take slow, deep breaths, grinding my teeth with the effort to move my hands, which are cramped like claws with my fingers curled from over an hour of gripping bricks. My heart leaps in my throat when a howl breaks the silence. It's answered by the hoot of an owl a moment later. The echoes of the sounds keep me company while I try to catch my breath and kick my butt into gear to get moving. More raindrops pepper my face and I roll to my belly before lifting up on all fours.

They keep an eye on me wherever I go inside the academy. This is the only way I can think of to follow the demon guards I've seen sneaking around. They all go up the wide stairways past the third floor disappearing from view. When I try to follow, a few of them get in my face and I have to fight them if I want to see where they are going. Making a quick decision, I back away from the fight—yeah, I know I was surprised as well—and this is what I come up with as an alternative. Climbing walls Spiderman style like an idiot.

Snorting at my stupidity, I get on my feet and look around the rooftop. The moon casts her silvery glow, breaking apart the shadows. There must be a way to get to this roof from the inside. The tiles look new, the dark gray color not faded or cracked. Either someone is maintaining them or they just use magic. Throwing a glance down to the pebbled path circling the building, my stomach drops in a free-style flip flop. If it's magic, I'm screwed. No way I'm climbing back down the way I came. I'll just sit here until someone finds me. I'll say I am sleepwalking, or something. I'm sure that will go as well as trying to pet a snake.

Rolling my shoulders to release the tension, I shake out my hands and hunch down, creeping closer to the other side of the roof. Stepping lightly on the angled tiles to not make a sound, I get as close to the edge as I can. A hum disturbing the air freezes my movements. Holding my breath and straining my ears, I inch closer, noticing for the first time a raised frame just to the left of where I'm crouched. It's either a door or a window but I couldn't care less. I feel like crying from excitement that I will eventually get out of here like a normal person and not a thief. The hum is slightly louder the closer I get, two distinct voices ringing clear in it. I can't make out any words yet, the darkened window reason enough for the sounds to be muffled. Pressing my knees on the hard tiles, hands braced on the frame on either side, I lean in as close as I dare without pressing my ear on the glass.

"What are we doing?"

Swallowing the scream that lodges in my throat at the hushed whisper next to my ear, my fist connects to a warm, unforgiving palm. Thick fingers wrap around my knuckles a second before my body tilts sideways, gravity pulling it straight toward the window. My eyes scrunch up as I brace for the impact. A muscular arm snakes around my waist, yanking me back into a broad chest and the scent of rain-forests and rain fills my nostrils. Clenching my jaw, I beg the fates for patience.

"This is how you get killed." Hissing under my breath, I open my eyes to glare at Fenrir.

"You were really sneaky, so I figured we need to be quiet." Placing me gently next to him and off his lap, the Fae leans over the window like he can see through the dark glass.

"I was sneaky so you wouldn't follow me around." Pushing the words out, I try my best not to yell at him. He tilts his face my way lifting one eyebrow in an unspoken question, *"How did that work out for you?"*

"How did you get here, Fenrir?" He doesn't look one bit tired, his hair smooth as silk while my braid looks like dogs have been gnawing on it while stray hairs stick to the sides of my face.

Not turning, he points behind him and I follow the direction of that one graceful finger to a small trap door gaping open a few feet behind us. I didn't even see it there. It takes everything in me not to whack him across the head, my body screaming at me in pain from the climb.

"What are we looking for here?" Murmuring under his breath, he tilts his head this way and that as if trying to catch a stray word through the thick glass. "Who's down there?"

"We were not looking for anything." Shoving him away with my shoulder, I kneel where I was before he came along. "I, on the other hand, was trying to see why the demons were sneaking up to the top floors and not letting anyone follow."

Eyeing the window frame, I trace my fingers around it to search for a latch, or anything really that will help me open it. Fenrir grunts something I don't hear, blowing a frustrated breath through his nose. It's funny now how I stupidly think I'll do anything without the Fae knowing about it.

"Let me see." After watching me for long moments, he pushes my hands away and nudges me out of my place. "I'm not sure these windows were meant to be opened." His lips barely move with the huffed words, a line forming between his eyebrows.

Chewing on my bottom lip, I glance from Fenrir to the open trap door and back. My body coils up and all my muscles stiffen, ready to spring into action. The Fae is fast, but I am faster. I can get through it and lock him out here if I time it right.

"I wouldn't do that if you don't want the demons to know you've been following them." Not looking away from his task, his tone is so soft I actually have to lean forward to hear his words. "If you lock me out, I'll break this window and catch you before you step foot out of the attic." An arrogant grin stretches his lips when he looks up. "Don't be so surprised, Hellion. I've watched you long enough to anticipate your actions."

"That's because you have stalker tendencies." Blowing out a breath, I keep my eyes locked on his, my mind spinning with ideas. No way I'm getting rid of him tonight. "Can you open it or not?" I sound snappy but the frustration is more from being unable to shake him off than anything else.

Without looking away, Fenrir's hands keep moving,

tracing the frame inside and out. A slow smile replaces the concentration on his face just as I hear the soft click. He winks at me before squeezing his fingers into the tiny gap and pulling the window silently open.

I stick my tongue out at him, which only widens his grin.

"… regardless of what you say. I think the timing is right," a deep voice grumbles from beneath us, pushing all other thoughts out of my head. I lean eagerly forward to hear better. "With all the shit going on, no one will be paying attention to us."

"I dunno about that," another one answers, followed by the shuffling of feet. "It might look like Alexius has the upper hand, but I wouldn't bet against Zoltan unless I see his head separated from his body. Do you really want to be the one standing in front of him answering why the book is missing if he survives?"

"You saw Zoltan led like a dog through the portal, yet here you are still afraid of him. I should've known you were a coward. I'll do it myself," the first demon snarls.

Fenrir snatches my arm to hold me in place. I'm not even aware I lift off my knees to jump down and kill the asshole for calling Zoltan a dog. Fury burns through my chest, my whole body trembling with the effort it takes to stay still. The Fae keeps his firm grip on my arm, but the look on his face is calm and collected.

"You are a fool." The voice of the second demon pulls me out of my murderous thoughts. "Don't look at me like that. You are an idiot if you think Zoltan is the only one you should be afraid of. Argoz and Fenrir will have your head if you get caught, as well as Astara. I don't even want to think what the half-blood will do."

My eyebrows crawl up my forehead all the way to my hairline. Fenrir's arm shakes slightly where he still holds me back, so I grab his wrist to prevent him from pouncing on the demons. I guess hearing them call me a half blood makes him upset. But then his shoulders start shaking too, so I angle myself to get a better look at his downturned face. The jerk is trying incredibly hard not to laugh. As if they have their own mind, my hands shoot out so I can punch the humor off his face. My finger bumps the slightly-opened window, my nail catching on a splinter of the weather-worn wood. The sharp piece stabs underneath my nail bed, crippling me in pain.

I grind my teeth.

"Did you hear that?" The second demon sounds alarmed, so I bite my lip even harder to ensure I don't scream, my eyes crossing from the throbbing of my finger.

"You really are a coward. First, a captured Daywalker makes you shake in fear, then a fucking girl scares you, and now even birds freak you out. You are a disgrace," the first demon spits angrily. "I'll get the book tomorrow night. Alexius is sending someone to pick it up in two days' time. You can explain then why you were sitting on your ass when everything we've ever wanted is within reach."

A door slams, and I jump out of my skin from the loud crash while Fenrir searches my face in concern. Swallowing the bile in my throat, I shove my forefinger in his face. Flinching, he rears back, his eyes crossing when he tries to see what I'm showing him. A tiny, sharp splinter is sticking out from under my short, blunt nail, the bigger part of it embedded in the nail bed. Tears gather at the corners of my eyes. The second demon mutters something intangible before we hear the door open and close again.

Fenrir folds his lips inward, biting on them hard.

My eyes narrow to slits.

"Let me see." Clearing his throat, he tries and fails to keep a straight face while reaching for my hand.

I say nothing when he takes my fingers in his, pinching the splinter between his thumb and forefinger. Clenching my jaw, I squeeze my eyes shut when he yanks it out. Another sharp pain stabs through me from the now-bleeding puncture, this one spearing all the way to my shoulder.

"I believe the humans call this instant karma." Holding the offending splinter like a trophy between us, the jerk grins so wide it looks like his face will split from it.

I punch him.

Sprawling on his back on the rooftiles, the Fae roars with laughter. His hair escapes the rubber band holding it at the base of his neck, the platinum strands contrasting against the dark gray tiles. Head thrown back, I watch his chest shake, the moon casting shadows and sharpening the line of his cheekbones. A snort escapes me when I shake my head at his antics.

He laughs harder, slapping his thigh with one large hand, and his eyes glitter with tears when he looks at me. It's been a long time since I've seen Fenrir laugh and the knot in my chest loosens at the sight. Plopping on my ass next to him, I giggle.

"It hurts like a bitch." Peeking at my nail, I can't see anything other than blood pooling under it.

"I should frame it." Still chuckling, Fenrir sits up holding the stupid splinter like his life depends on it. "Nothing can make agent Drake blink an eye, but this splinter made her almost pass out."

"You are such a jerk. I did not almost pass out." Shoving him away by the shoulder, my eyes drift back to the slightly-opened window. "We have a lead, Fenrir."

He locks his gaze on mine, the too-blue color of his eyes looking as silver as the giant orb in the sky matching the moonlight. All the humor is gone as we stare at each other. It's been days since Roberti took Zoltan and we did nothing but chase our tails the entire time. We have no idea where to look, what to look for, or who to ask.

Myst, the strange female I met when I crossed the portal to the human world, disappeared after the hunters that night and I haven't heard anything from her either. Despair is eating a hole inside me as I think about what may be happening to Zoltan all while I sit here doing nothing. I've been avoiding Astara as well, because I can't look at her. I'm too afraid I'll see disgust and betrayal in her gaze.

Until now.

"I'll tell Argoz…"

"Don't you dare say a word to anyone." Hissing at him, I take a fistful of his shirt and yank his face to mine. His eyes widen comically. 'No one hears about this; do you understand me? I will wait in the library to see what book Alexius needs. If he needs it, I want it more. The demon will lead us to his contact and that will take us to Zoltan. If you screw this up with your rules or whatever, I'll skin you, Fae."

"I was only suggesting a backup, Francesca." Lifting both hands in surrender, he frowns at me. "I want to find him as much as you do, but we don't know who this contact is. You can't help Zoltan if you are dead, or taken away just like him."

"You can come." My hand twists his shirt tighter. "No one else Fenrir. I'm not planning to engage; I'm going to follow."

"Even through the portal." He searches my eyes as understanding dawns on him. "You think they'll lead you to

Zoltan. It's a risky move and hardly the case. It sounds too easy."

"Would you or anyone you know have done it?"

"No." As he answers, his eyebrows shoot up.

"Exactly. Alexius knows how you think. He doesn't know shit about me." Releasing his shirt, I stand up on my feet, slapping dust from my pants. "Unless Roberti has spilled his guts—and he is not one to share what he knows —they don't know what I'll do. I'll see you tomorrow."

"Where are you going now?"

"To get some sleep." I feel his eyes on me until I disappear through the trap door. My mind is spinning with worry and excitement.

Finally, a lead.

Instigated: Chapter Two

Zoltan stands stock still, fists clenched, and a muscle jumping angrily on his chiseled jaw. Alex and Cassius flank him on either side, both holding daggers dripping with black poison under his chin. His entire body is vibrating in rage, but he doesn't move. When I see Cassius's daughter standing right behind them with a hand pressed on Alex's back, everything becomes clear. All the fighting has stopped, and everyone is staring at the entrance of the portal. A hunter thrusts his blade at my chest, but I spin, grabbing his arm and wrenching it out of his socket. The hunter screams a bloodcurdling sound when his arm dangles in my hand. I drop it at my feet, my eyes never leaving Zoltan's.

"I knew you had it in you, Franky." I recoil from Andrius's voice a second before he steps through the portal.

Dark energy comes off him in waves, darkness dancing like a living cloak around his shoulders. Moving closer to where they hold Zoltan, his gaze traces my body slowly up and down, lingering on the exposed glimpse of my breasts. Bile rises in the back of my throat.

Another hunter inches closer from my side. My arm shoots out, my fingers gripping his throat and my nails digging into his windpipe. My hand curls, sinking into flesh, blood drenching it to my wrist. I open my fingers, releasing the blob in my hand to follow the crumbling body of the gurgling hunter to the ground.

"She is magnificent." Andrius claps his hands in glee, his eyes glittering with madness. "Isn't she?"

"It's me you want, Roberti." Taking a step closer, I ignore Zoltan's glare. "Let him go."

"Why should I do that?" He sounds like we are discussing the price of potatoes at the market. Anger bubbles in my chest. "When I can have you both?"

"You'll have a lot of dead hunters and might even lose your useless life if you don't let him go." Sliding my feet on the floor, I inch closer. "If you think I'll come willingly after you hurt him, you are crazier than I thought."

"I won't hurt him." Andrius, in his right mind, slaps Zoltan's face good-naturedly. My chest vibrates from the vampire's growl. "He is leverage."

"Why are you doing this?" I think I see Leo's tail slinking on the side, but I can't be sure. I slide closer. "What is it you want?"

"It's not what I want, Drake." His face twists in anger. "It's what everyone wants. Don't you see?" Spreading his arm around, he points at the people around us. "Who decided that vampires are the top of the food chain, that the rest of us should crawl at their feet? You think the shifters and the demons don't loathe being guards. Being treated like the dirt under their shoe. Well"—He grins with no humor —"let's see them now. There is a bigger power in town."

"That's it? You are doing this for your ego, you stupid fuck?" I see a hunter creeping closer from the corner of my eye, but I'm too angry to care. "You are killing innocents in Sienna, and in the academy, so you can feel important. You really are a moron, you know that right?"

"You'll see things my way soon enough, Drake," Andrius snarls.

"*Now get your ass through the portal, or it'll go down. Alex was smart enough to get enough of your blood to bring all the portals down. Let's see how you feel knowing it's you that is responsible for so many deaths.*"

"*You will not pin this on me.*" But his words stab me in the chest. What the shifter said to me in the dining room rings in my ears. "*It's all her fault.*"

"*Don't listen to him.*" Fenrir materializes next to me, his power holding by a thin thread that's ready to explode and knock us all over. "*He is full of shit.*"

"*Should I kill him now, and we fight?*" Andrius leans forward in anticipation. "*What do you say, Fenrir? With Zoltan dead, you can have her all to yourself.*" He leers at me, making my skin crawl.

"*He won't kill him,*" a woman's voice hisses to my right and I stiffen when I catch a glimpse of white clothing. "*He's bluffing, don't be stupid. Let him take him; you can get him out.*" It sounds so familiar it takes a moment to place it.

"*What the fuck?*" hissing under my breath, I'm grateful Andrius is focused on the Fae at the moment. "*Myst?*"

"*I got you, chica. That asshat manipulated me, as well. I knew Alex was up to something.*" She inches closer, raising all the red flags in my head. Fenrir says something I don't hear.

"*And I should trust you, why?*" Everything is so messed up right now I want to scream until my throat is raw.

"*You shouldn't.*" She snickers like a nutcase. "*But the enemy of my enemy is my friend. He won't kill the hunk. But he can bring the portals down.*"

"*Fuck me.*" I breathe and she snorts.

"*You're hot and all, but I don't swing that way.*" When Fenrir fidgets next to me, I know he can hear us and that my time is up.

"*What will it be, Drake?*" Andrius glows in glee. "*The Daywalker or Sienna?*"

"Zoltan!"

The scream is ripped from my chest when I bolt straight up in bed, drenched in cold sweat. Tears stream down my cheeks, soaking my hair and pillow. Every night is the same thing. Every time I close my eyes, I relive that horrible scene over and over with the same result.

They always take him away.

The door is nearly ripped off the hinges, banging loudly off the opposite wall before swinging back and almost hitting Fenrir in the face. He lifts his arm, palm slapping it away as he rushes to my side. I want to laugh, but breathing is such a struggle at the moment that I can't. My heart hammers in my ribcage with a vengeance. The Fae whirls around, knees bending as if he expects to find someone attacking me. He's been patrolling every night, but I think this is the first time he has witnessed my nightmares.

"I'm fine, Fenrir. No one is there." Gasping the words out, I pull the sheet up to my neck. The white tank top I'm wearing is see through from the wet patches all over it. The last thing I need is to flash my nipples at the Fae.

Fenrir turns around slowly and straightens. His gaze searches my face and a line forms between his arched eyebrows. Not wanting him to see how unsettled the dreams make me, I glance around the room, my eyes landing on random things just so I don't look at him. My fingers hurt from how hard I'm squeezing the sheets at my chest.

"I didn't know you were having nightmares." With a sigh, he lowers to the edge of the bed, the mattress dipping under his weight while his eyes remain glued on me. "I should've known."

"You're not my mother, Fae, nor am I a child. We all relive our failures when you do what we do." I hate that I sound defensive, and I hate even more that he has a sad look plastered on his face. "I don't need you to feel sorry for me, Fenrir. Or responsible, for that matter." Offering him a smile I don't feel, I try to take the sting away from my words. "I'm a big girl. I can handle a few nightmares."

"You know you can trust me, right?" He tugs on my hand a few times before I allow him to take it in his. His thumb rubs soothing circles over the back of it, and I feel my shoulders lower slightly. They were up to my ears from tension.

A harsh snort through my nose is his answer.

"I'm not your enemy, Hellion …"

"Neither are you a friend."

"I know you've been left on your own your entire life but that doesn't have to be the case anymore." He watches me intently, ignoring my previous comment. "You don't have to talk to me about it, but you let Astara in. She is your friend so talk to her."

"About what? That because of me her brother might be dead already? I'm sure that conversation will go well." Yanking my hand back, I curl my knees and wear my arms around them. "I don't need therapy, Fenrir, or to talk things through. That's what humans do. We go kill the fuckers that won't let us sleep." When he keeps staring at me and says nothing, I sigh, deflating. "What?"

"I was going to talk to you about it tomorrow at break-fast"—Swinging his legs up, he gets comfortable by stretching out on my bed, his feet crossing at the ankles next to my hips—"but since we both can't sleep let's make the most of it."

My face twists in a grimace to show him how ecstatic I am about his idea, but I wiggle sideways to give him more room. One cheek jumping in a barely contained smile, he slides closer and leans on one elbow, making himself at home. I have a feeling this is going to be a long night.

"Well? Out with it and maybe I'll get an hour of sleep before everyone starts making noise around here."

"Let me see your finger." Lifting his palm up, his fingers wiggle in expectation for me to do what he asked.

"It healed, I wasn't stabbed in the kidney. Just a stupid splinter." But I do place my fingers in his, letting him turn the said finger this way and that to inspect it. "See? I'll live, unfortunately."

"Hmmm." Shaking his head, his platinum strands slide over his shoulders like silk as he offers me a grim look. "I'm not sure anyone can survive this, Drake. It was, after all, a vicious splinter bred to kill."

I try.

I try with everything in me not to laugh but after a few snorts, bursts of laughter have me clutching my stomach from the serious expression on his face. The corners of his lips twitch a few times too before he joins me, chuckling as well.

"You are such a goof, Fae." Gasping for air, I straighten as a few more giggles pass my lips. "Now that we settled my impending doom named death by a splinter, can I hear what you want to talk about?"

Leaning back, he runs his fingers through his hair, pushing it back over his shoulders. I can see he is thinking how to phrase whatever it is he wants to say. I've been more hotheaded than usual lately because fear for Zoltan's life, for the portals, and everything else is making my head spin. I don't blame him for walking on eggshells around me. I would slap some sense into my own head if I was in his shoes.

Good thing he knows better than to try.

"I've been observing you ever since I saw you in the bar in Sienna." Referring to the night when I visited my friend

Daren's bar in hopes to get drunk and drown my sorrows, Fenrir brings back memories I'd rather forget.

I was suspended from the Special Forces for the Accord where I worked as an agent under Roberti. Fenrir apparently was there to check out who he would be dealing with in person. I brushed him off, storming out of the bar and spending a good amount of time that night riding my bike through Sienna aimlessly to clear my head. It was the night I was assigned to infiltrate the academy. It was also when everything went to shit.

"It's nice to have time to sit back and observe while the rest of us are fighting for our lives." I flinch at my comment because I said it out of spite and to shake off the feelings that came with thinking about how naïve I was. "I didn't mean that."

"I know you didn't." Scratching his jaw, he eyes me contemplatively. "That just supports my observations actually. You see we know now that Roberti was playing the long game, especially with you. While we were too busy with distractions, which I have no doubt he orchestrated, he was placing all the chess pieces on the board. Lucky for us, and very unfortunate for him, he underestimated you just like everyone else."

"I have no idea what that means," I tell him honestly, pointing a finger at his face. "I will never be a pawn as long as I breathe."

"No, you were never meant as a pawn." I almost thank him, but he ruins it with his next words. "In his game of chess, you are meant as the queen." A grin spreads across his face at my scowl. "What he didn't expect was for the queen to start kicking like the knight, tracking him like the bishop, and blasting him like the rook."

"I don't play chess, Fenrir. I'm too busy surviving. Get to your point."

"That's exactly it, Drake." His hand flicks at me as he speaks, all the muscles in his arm jumping under his skin and distracting me for a second. The Fae needs to be less attractive if he wants anyone to actually pay attention to what he is saying. By the knowing grin he shoots me, he is aware of my exact thoughts in this moment, too. The jerk.

"Roberti thought by giving you his protection he would mold you into an obedient soldier for his cause. He never expected your trust issues to be so rooted that what you showed him would only be a small facet of who and what you really were. A mask, albeit a real part of Francesca Drake. His arrogance will be his downfall."

"And what? You think you know the real Francesca?" A sharp ping of fear spears through me but I don't show it, instead keeping my face impassive. "I don't even know who or what I am."

"Far from it, but I'm slowly learning. Before you try to bite my head off, let me finish." I press my lips closed hard because I almost tell him what I think about his learning. "As I said, I think that played well for us to even tweak his plans as much as we have so far. But it's not enough and I think you'll do much better—we will all do much better if we train you properly on how to use your powers. You do astoundingly well by acting on instinct and impulse. I must say I'm impressed, but you lack discipline. I'm worried that it'll cost you in the long run."

"I ..." His eyes turn into slits when I open my mouth, knowing before I do that I am going to talk shit just for the sake of pissing him off. My mouth closes with an audible click, my nostrils flaring.

"I'm not going to say you're not right in your *observation* because we both know you excel in your stalker tendencies. Stop smiling, though. It's creepy as fuck." No amount of glaring can wipe the smirk off his pretty face. "Anyway, we don't have time to train or whatever else you have in mind, Fenrir. Thanks to that asshole Alex, they have a lot of my blood to mess with the portals, plus they have Zoltan. We can't sit behind these walls playing training camp. Not now."

"True." Giving me a very royal-like incline of his head, I can see the wheels turning behind his eyes. "That's why I have an offer for you, Hellion. One I think you will like." He rushes to assure me when I fill my lungs to speak.

"What kind of an offer, Fenrir? If I know anything about the Fae, that's to never make a deal with one. You'll always get screwed at the end." After I realize what word I just used, I stab a finger at his nose. "Don't even go there. There will be no screwing with anyone."

"Such a prude." But he laughs, proving he loves pissing me off as much as I love doing it to him. "I will not cage you inside these walls. That was never my intention. But instead of aimlessly searching for leads and sneaking around, we can use that time to strengthen your powers while looking for Zoltan. I will train you myself. Leo offered as well."

We look at each other with our gazes locked for a long time. On one hand, I know he is right. All this time I've been winging it, using whatever comes to me on its own to survive the situations I am thrown in. On the other, urgency is stabbing like the claws of a beast in my chest to get to Zoltan because time is running out. My head is spinning with indecision, and I want to say "let's do it" at the same time as I tell him "no way am I training now." Fenrir startles my by jumping off the bed and striding to the door before I can realize what he is doing.

"We start right after breakfast. Sleep well." Throwing it over his shoulder, he closes the door before I can protest, leaving me with my mouth open and a million curses I don't get to say.

Grab your copy…
vinci-books.com/instigated